The ANTI HERO

RENEE ROCCO

THE ANTIHERO

Copyright © 2024 by Renee Rocco
All rights reserved.

No part of this book may be reproduced in any form or by any electronic or mechanical means, including information storage and retrieval systems, without written permission from the author, except for the use of brief quotations in a book review.

This is a work of fiction. Names, characters, businesses, places, events, locales, and incidents are either the products of the author's imagination or used in a fictitious manner. Any resemblance to actual persons, living or dead, or actual events is purely coincidental.

Cover Design: Renee Rocco
Interior Design: Renee Rocco
Proofreader: Lisa Gilliam

First Electronic Edition: May 2024
First Print Edition: May 2024

Printed in the United States of America

CONTENT ADVISORY

Welcome to my imagination, where the villains often tend to be the heroes. Although meant as a fun, light read, this story includes subject matter that may trigger some readers.

Graphic sex
Parental death (FMC off-page, in the past)
Miscarriage (FMC, off-page, in the past)
Divorce (FMC, off-page, in the past)
Child loss (secondary character, off-page, in the past)

For Mommy Bunny.

There was no conflict, and that's the truth. You were the first person I saw, the first person I loved, and I will miss you every day until I close my eyes for the last time. Thank you for making me strong. I hope I made you proud.

FORWARD

I want to take a moment to thank Brooklyn Cross, Harley Laroux, Nikki St. Crowe, and Molly Doyle for allowing me to use their names and/or their books as Easter eggs throughout *THE ANTIHERO*. Even casually knowing these talented (and totally badass) authors is an honor and a pleasure, and I hope I've done their generosity and trust justice.

Each book in The Book Boyfriends series is a self-aware love letter to the romance community. From the cinnamon-est of rolls to the anti-est of heroes, I want to honor the characters and tropes that have given me such joy—with a dash of humor, a drizzle of sappiness, and a heavy sprinkle of sarcasm, of course!

I adore this wonderful community we've created, and I'm grateful that you picked mine out of all the awesome book choices out there! May you have as much fun reading *THE ANTIHERO* as I had writing Charlotte and Rhys's story!

—Renee, xoxox

PLAYLIST

Antihero by Taylor Swift
willow by Taylor Swift
Cruel Summer by Talyor Swift
Beautiful Things by Benson Boone
Only You by Joshua Radin
What If You by Joshua Radin
abcdefu by GAYLE
Leave a Light On by Papa Roach
Cupid by Sam Cooke
Cry to Me by Solomon Burke
Demons by Imagine Dragon
Party Your Body by Stevie B
Unwritten by Natasha Bedingfield
When Will I See You Again by The Three Degrees

ONE

This is a bunch of bullshit.

No, seriously, I'm already done dealing with Jason, and he only just got here. My right eye is twitching, forcing me to apply pressure—using my middle finger, of course—to my temple. Sure, it's a futile effort to make it stop. And sure, I absolutely could have used my index finger, but it's the tiny victories that count. A subtle 'fuck you' to the man I once loved.

We were together for ten years, married for seven of them. We were always oil and water, but I desperately tried to be someone I wasn't so I could blend into him—to be the best wife possible. I was under the foolish assumption that what Jason Wembley and I had was real—right up to the day I learned there were three of us in our marriage.

Jason, Lisa Edgar, and lastly me.

Cheating on me for six years wasn't enough for Mr. Small Town Golden Boy. Oh, no. Once he ripped out my heart, he proceeded to shit on the bloody remains. And then he moved Lisa into the house he and I had lived in during our marriage, the one I'd picked out and lovingly furnished—and lost in the divorce settlement.

So, that was fun.

Mr. High School Quarterback never wanted to marry me. Apparently, I was a high school fling that lasted too long. I robbed years of his life when I got pregnant, and his family forced us to get married. Even now, he's not done making me suffer for 'stealing' that time from him.

See, the thing is, the Wembleys frown upon divorce. Heaven forbid their 'good' name is besmirched here in Harley Cove—a.k.a. Perfectville, USA. Instead, they pressured us to marry at twenty years old, and I went along with their ridiculous plan because my only family is my grandmother, whose advice was, *"Charly, a gal can do worse than those Wembleys."*

Yeah, but not by much, I learned.

And that's how I, poor-ass nobody, Charlotte Allison Mallory, got myself hitched to the wealthiest family in Wayne County, Pennsylvania.

It should have been quite the fairytale, right? A sad-sack girl from the wrong side of the tracks makes good with her quarterback-boyfriend-turned-husband. What a storybook tale, right? Wrong. That's the exact opposite of what happened in real life.

Jason's mom, Lydia, pressured me to quit college, and like an idiot, I listened, dropping out right after I learned I was pregnant.

Then came our rushed wedding, where his nasty family whispered "gold-digger" and "trash" behind my back.

I lost the baby two months later.

No one knows why. It was simply one of those things—one of those cruel blows from Mother Nature. I should have walked away from Jason right then and there. Ran away, actually. But I stayed. Why? I was a silly girl who believed I was in love despite a marriage decorated in red flags. Still, I stayed...

...until I caught this piece of shit red-handed, fucking Lisa in our bed.

Yeah, no, he couldn't lie his way out of that one.

Fending off the beginnings of a migraine, I stop massaging my temple but keep glaring at Jason. *Jason-fucking-Wembley*, with his coifed hair and cruel eyes. I wanted to be the woman who mussed that blonde mop and wrinkled his crisp, expensive suits. Now, I'm standing here, envisioning myself choking him to death with that gray-and-blue checkered tie.

"To what do I owe the pleasure of your esteemed visit to my bookshop?"

That your money bought me, asshole.

Our shitty marriage wasn't a total loss. I walked away with a glorious divorce settlement.

Jason glares down his imperial nose at me like I'm still the fragile teenager he can intimidate. Wow, yeah, that's not me anymore. I grew the fuck up, and as for him... The strain of being married to me did him dirty—as if I was the problem.

Me—his devoted wife who cooked and cleaned and ensured his whole damn world ran in perfect order down to the tiniest detail.

While I was busy tending to our life, he was building a future with Lisa.

But, sure, I was the problem. The shrew who trapped him with a baby.

He can fuck right off with the bullshit he's been spewing for the past year since I caught him with his dick in that woman.

Totally out of place in the cozy backdrop of The Scorched Page, Jason is dressed in a typically expensive suit with blond hair coiffed to death. He stands ramrod straight to maximize his solid, six-foot stature. He's a handsome man, but his shitty personality makes him ugly. You can see his merciless soul reflected in his ice-blue eyes. And he's still drenching himself in that awful aftershave, the one he thinks makes him smell like old money but actually makes him reek of old man.

"Since you're going to hear it around town, I thought it best if you heard it from me first."

Oh, great, another announcement. Fun. The last newsflash he delivered was to tell me Lisa was moving into my old house. "Let me guess, you and Lisa are getting married." At his nod, I give him a snarky round of applause. "Congrats. When's the wedding?"

Jason flares his nostrils, sniffing the air like there's an old fish or something rotting behind the register. He lifts his chin in that arrogant way that makes me want to see how hard I have to punch him to crack that weak jawline. "Next month."

"Wow," I breathe, hiding my cringe because I sound exactly like Owen Wilson. "Why the rush?"

But even as I ask the question, I guess the answer. "We're expecting."

No shit.

I curl my lips around my teeth and rock back on the heels of my Doc Martens. Suddenly, I'm every bit the mountain mud girl all over again, the one who was orphaned at seven and who was so poor, I slept on my grandmother's couch. I'd have had my own room, maybe even a cot or something, but her shack over on St. Crowe Lake is a teeny one-bedroom and she needs to sleep on one of those in-home medical beds. There was simply no space, so we made do.

But I shake off the sensation and remember I'm not the sad and lonely little girl anymore. I've come a long way from those days. Who cares if Wembley money lifted me out of poverty? I made the most of the opportunity. That's what matters.

Running my palms down the skirt of my pink sundress, I nod thoughtfully before saying, "How awesome. Congrats on this joyous news as well." I offer him the most bullshit smile I have ever smiled in the history of smiles. "I'm happy for you and Lisa. Truly."

My toes are crossed inside my shoes.

I wish the *baby* well.

Jason and Lisa can go fuck themselves.

Perhaps I'd be more charitable toward them if Jason didn't use every opportunity to publicly bad-mouth me. We've been apart for a year. I keep to my quiet corner of Harley Cove while he struts around town, spreading lies about me to anyone who will listen. How I was a nagging wife who was terrible in bed. What a jerkoff, living his dream life while I'm made out to be the villain in his perfectly constructed story.

Did I expect it to play differently?

Not really.

Jason Wembley is Harley Cove's golden boy. I'm its former troubled child who married above my station. This whole town probably rejoiced when Jason finally shed me like a bad habit. He and Lisa are better suited for each other. They fit. She's the ideal trophy wife, a former Miss Harley Cove. The woman is tall, platinum-blonde, and has sparkling blue eyes. A living doll with a thin body tailor-made for designer clothes and a flawless face.

I'm the anti-Lisa. Five-four on a tall day. Brown curls. Green eyes. My body type is best described as 'I'm eating that slice of cake.' My sense of style is the nineties, thank you very much. I don't see myself as beautiful, but others do, and I'm grateful for their compliments because getting cheated on for six years was a mind fuck of monumental proportions.

"Thank you." Jason's voice was the one thing I never did like about him. It's not…masculine. Not deep enough. Not gravelly. There's zero baritone. I've always liked something…smoky. Something rich. Not something slightly nasal and a tad too high. But, hey, he's not mine anymore. I don't have to suffer his annoying ass anymore, thank God. He's Lisa's problem now—until death do they part (or he finds a newer, younger, and prettier model). "You're… Um, that is to say…" He licks his lips, and I'm flabbergasted that the unflappable Jason Wembley is, in fact, flapped. "Lisa and I… My mother, as well… It's best if you…"

I nail my hands to my hips and blow out an exasperated sigh. I know what he's stammering about, and if I want to, I can make this easy on him. "Yes? What is it, Jason? I don't understand."

Given the current situation, I'm not feeling overly charitable.

"You won't be invited, of course." God forbid Jason shoves his hands, with their manicured nails, into the pockets of his pristine navy suit. "We feel it will be best if you don't make a case out of it."

I want to laugh, I really do. The giggle is there, sitting on the tip of my tongue, threatening to burst forth. Why in the world would I *ever* want to attend my ex-husband's wedding? More precisely, why would I want to attend his wedding to the woman he was cheating on me with?

His *shotgun* wedding to the woman he was cheating on me with. He's wildly delusional and god-awfully full of himself.

But also, the thing about the Wembleys is that they value saving face above everything else. When we got married, only his parents knew I was pregnant. Everyone else saw us as impatient sweethearts eager to kick-start our lives together. We remained married because—*God forbid*—the Wembleys had a divorce in their family. Hell no. Those people stay married no matter what. Through cheating, abuse, whatever. Everything but love binds them, and when Jason and I formally announced we were going our separate ways, I darkened their good name in a way that can never be forgiven or forgotten.

Even now, if I see a Wembley around town, I either get a dirty look, or they pretend I don't exist.

I prefer the latter.

However, we collectively play the Everything Is Awesome game, to the outside world. No one beyond his family knows Jason cheated on me. Public perception is that we *tragically* grew apart…as sometimes happens with adolescent love. We pretend we're the dearest of friends, despite the nonchalant way he besmirches me to anyone with fucking ears. But look at us, how sweet, getting along.

Aw!

Except we can't be in the same room for longer than three minutes without wanting to murder each other.

"No worries, babe. The last thing in the world I want to do is watch you marry her. But I thank you for taking the time out of your obviously busy day to come here to tell me the news personally." With a little spin, I gesture at the fresh delivery of boxes that arrived this morning. "I'm sure we *both* have things we'd rather be doing than this." I motion from him, then to myself. "So…"

Jason, who has never stepped a single foot inside The Scorched Page, sweeps his critical gaze around my cozy bookshop. At the inviting coffee station near the huge front window, where bold, vintage black lettering spells out the shop's name. He takes a quick stroll. Drags his fingers along the spines of a row of books that I lovingly curated and carefully placed on the walnut shelves lining the wood-paneled walls. In a small town that already has a general bookstore, I wanted something different. A place dedicated to romance, where not only sweet once upon a times and happily ever afters are found, but also the darkest of taboos. Those love stories deserve space as well.

Leave it to my ex to discover the filthiest book in the shop. He slides it off the shelf, the cover innocuous enough. Dark. Gothic. Just a simple skull and some dark flowers. A solid white title reads: *Shout for Us*. Jason turns the book over. Scans the back blurb, a scowl drawing his threaded brows together. God, I've always hated that expression. A fight always followed. He opens the book to a random page. That frown morphs into shock mixed with a layer of disgust.

"Really, Charly?" He slams the book closed and tosses it on a nearby table that rests next to a red wing-backed chair. "This is the garbage you sell? You bought a porn shop with my money?"

Taken aback, I literally take a fucking step back. "First, it was *my* money. Mine. I earned it by having to put up with your bullshit for ten years. Six of which you were screwing another woman. So, yeah, you don't have the right to take a moral fucking stance with me, you dirty cheater. Second, no one has a problem when a certain author writes about kids having sex in the same book where a demon disguises itself as a clown to eat children. But when women write sex-positive books? Oh, my gawd. Garbage! Porn! We must protect the children!" I roll my eyes and let out a snorting laugh. "Please. Get real. And while you're at it, get the hell out."

Jason, true to form, notches his cleft chin. "This is why our marriage was such an epic failure."

I blink innocently at him, having never minded our height differences until now. "And here I thought it was because three's a crowd."

"No, Charlotte, it's because I could never love a foul-mouthed bitch like you."

Even a year ago, those words would have destroyed me. Today, however… I wipe the back of my hand across my forehead. "Whew! Thank God for small miracles. I'd hate to be the sort of bitch a piece of shit like you could love. That would make me a superficial, home-wrecking sexbot."

"Lisa is a good woman."

I'm almost proud of Jason for defending his fiancée, but I beg to differ. "You and I have vastly different definitions for *good*." I surround the word in air quotes.

"How would you know? You never took the time to get to know her."

"Oh!" I pull a cringe face and slap a hand over my heart. "My bad. Was I supposed to? Damn. I must have missed the lesson on proper etiquette regarding a husband's infidelity when your mother taught me how to be a perfect Wembley wife." I gesture with my finger as I ask, "Did it come before or after she called me a whore and demanded I get a paternity test when we told her I was pregnant?"

Jason's sneer is absurdly haughty for a man who lives off his family's wealth and privilege without earning it himself. "I didn't come here to argue."

"Cool, same," I snap. "I don't want to argue, either."

"Then don't be argumentative."

"Then don't be spiteful."

"I wasn't," he grinds out between gritted teeth.

Snorting, I roll my eyes. "Bullshit. You're a grown-ass man, Jason. One who got handed the position of COO of his daddy's company. You have always controlled every word that oozes out of the hole in your face. So again, if you don't want to see the worst side of me, don't bring the worst side of you. Deal?" I hold out my hand for him to shake.

He stares at my peace offering as if my hand is smeared with feces.

I drop my arm.

"Once an asshole, always an asshole," I mutter.

"Have a nice life, Charly."

"Trust me, pal, I am," I say with a big, bright grin as Jason spins on the heels of his polished black shoes—shoes that undoubtedly cost more than every article of clothing in my entire closet combined. His steps don't falter as he marches his arrogant self toward the door. Not even when I shout, "Keep those checks coming, Moneybags."

The nickname was a joke when we were teenagers.

He called me Rags.

Obviously, it was a play on our wealth inequality. Back then, I innocently thought it was hilarious. As an adult, I understand why I should have never found it funny.

Jason had the power in our relationship—until I divorced him. Now, thanks to the beauty of alimony, he has to pay me a king's ransom as punishment for him having been a shitty husband. Oh, yeah, you bet your sweet ass I made sure he feels the sting every time he writes those checks. Hell, I hired the best lawyer his money could buy. Grabbed Donald J. Ralston before Jason could, and that shark went in for the kill.

When the little brass bell above the door chimes, signaling Jason's departure from The Scorched Page, I breathe a sigh of relief. That entitled jerkoff uses too much space he doesn't deserve. With a slap of my palms against my thighs and a little shrug, I head to the coffee station, grateful for the quiet and calm in the wake of his departure.

Do I care he's marrying Lisa? No. Like Thanos, their marriage was inevitable. I don't even care that she's pregnant. What I do care about is that I want him to leave me the hell alone. Stop talking about me. Stop lying about me. Leave me to live my life and let our past die.

After making myself a much-needed cup of coffee, I pick up the discarded copy of *Shout for Us* by Holly Boyle.

Great book by a brilliant author.

Rather than slide it back on the shelf, I bring it to my office—which is a MacBook Pro next to the register. I shove the book in my tote bag hanging off the back of my comfy leather desk chair. I guess it's time for a reread. What can I say? Dark romance is my safe space. I won't apologize for it, never have, and never will.

Long live the antihero and enemies-to-lovers trope.

No, but seriously, I've always been a reader, and I can't imagine my life without books. Hence, why it was almost a compulsion to open The Scorched Page. A calling, if you will, and if Jason ever again refers to these books as garbage, I'm going to beat him half to death with one. Because the beauty of divorce means I don't have to play nice when he pulls his pompous behavior bullshit.

I glance at my tote, winking at the book tucked inside it. "Nope, we certainly don't, do we?" I ask it as if the characters written on those pages can—and will—answer me. "And it's at this point in the story when Charly realizes she seriously needs a social life that consists of more than fictional men and a vibrator."

Because that's been the extent of my social interaction ever since my epic split from Harley Cove's resident golden boy. But I'm going to get out there. Get back on the figurative horse. Maybe do something wild and hop on an actual man and ride him like an actual horse. I don't know. We'll see where this whole fraternizing thing goes. I'm twenty-eight, not eighty-eight. Time for me to stop living like an old hermit and enjoy life. We only get one chance at it, and I'm watching mine pass me by.

I grab my cell phone off the counter and do the typical scroll, finding no new emails or notifications on my socials. Not a shocker there. One must be social on the apps to receive social interaction.

Funny thing about apps...

I swear phones can read a person's mind, because an ad for an app pops up, and while my initial instinct is to scroll past it, I stop. Maybe because The Book Boyfriends seems like harmless fun. A silly way to kill time. After a glance around the empty shop and a one-shoulder shrug, I tap the Download Now button because...

Why not?

No big deal.

The moment The Book Boyfriends finishes downloading, my phone pings its usual alert. I launch the app, and... *Wow*. It's a cheerful bright pink, almost to the point of burning the eyeballs. First, I create the requisite account. Then I build a profile and scroll through the possible 'boyfriends.' Options include, but are not limited to, Cinnamon Roll, Hockey Player, Billionaire, Demon, Antihero, Knight in Shining Armor, Mafia Boss, Monster, Best Friend, and Vampire. All undeniably interesting choices. However, one stands out from the crowd, and when I swipe right, there he is.

The Antihero.

Name: Rhys Ravenstone.

Not going to lie, I have a blast 'building' him, starting with his height. Six-feet-five because that seems like how tall an antihero should be. Dark hair. Dark eyes. Big ol' dick. Two hundred fifty pounds of muscle. Now, let's add tattoos. I tap my chin, pondering...

"What else are we giving you, Ravenstone?" A devious grin curls my lips. No self-respecting antihero is complete without a rather...interesting...piercing. "Sorry, my dude, but this one's gonna hurt."

One final touch. A scar. Gotta have a scar. A diagonal slash across his left cheek under his eye. Perfect! Moving on to the personality section. *Pfft.* This is easy. Loyalty is a must. Protective, *check*. Dangerous, *absolutely*. Let's add a heavy dose of arrogance. Has to be gruff, a man of few words, because antiheroes are notorious for one-word sentences. Oh! And the eyebrow thing. Dudes in books always lift a single brow and it's super sexy. Profession. Assassin, of course. I mean, go big or go home, right?

Should I be having this much fun?

Again, why not? It's a silly app—owned by...

Cupid.

Of course.

What's next? Is Thor going to launch a weather app?

When I'm done, the screen explodes with pink hearts. A cartoon version of Cupid shooting arrows follows. Next is the photo I uploaded of myself when building my profile, wiggling to the center of the screen. It's met halfway by a composite photo of my book boyfriend. Once they meet in the middle, the two photos overlap. A giant red heart encircles them, followed by the flashing words:

YOU'RE IN LUCK. YOU'VE BEEN STRUCK.
IS IT LOVE AT FIRST SIGHT OR LOVE AT FIRST FIGHT?
SEVEN DAYS TO BIND THE HEART
OR FOREVER BE KEPT APART.

"Yeah, yeah," I drawl with a wave of my hand. "Sorry, Cupid, but I've been in love, and you know what? It sucked. Never again. Next guy I meet, I don't care who he is." I wiggle my phone. "Not even Mr. Ravenstone here. I'm in it for a good time, not a long time."

Love.

What a fucking scam. Don't need it. Don't want it. Got no time for it. Not that it matters. Cupid is about as real as Rhys Ravenstone.

And on that note, time to get back to work because I've wasted enough time on this bullshit.

TWO

He skated his fingers along her spine, sending a delicious frisson of electricity dancing across her flesh. Heat flooded her, her desire pooling between her legs, drenching her red-lace panties. Greedy for more, she grabbed his wrist, forced his hand—

"Oof, sorry, babe, I gotta stop him right here." I slam *Shout for Us* closed. "After the shit day I had, I'm in no mood to read about you and what's his name doing the sexy time."

Digging my hand into a gigantic bowl of popcorn (I may or may not have added a ton of chocolate chips), I toss more than a comfortable handful in my mouth. I'm trying not to choke to death as I chew, ruminating about the fictional man I built on the silly book boyfriend app.

I have officially sunk to a whole new depth of pathetic.

No, seriously.

In my defense, Jason and I hadn't had sex in…let me do a quick tally…

About a year and three months prior to the divorce. I moved out exactly fourteen months ago. My vagina probably has cobwebs by now. In fact, fantasizing about a cartoon man is the least of my sexual problems. I bet it'd take a crowbar and a jug of lube to crank open this dusty canal.

What a catch, aren't I? Chilling on the couch in my favorite black yoga pants and a humongous yellow T-shirt with a salsa stain. With legs outstretched on the coffee table, I have Taylor Swift playing on Spotify. Two songs ago, I belted out "Willow" as if Taylor needed my help with vocals.

Newsflash, she didn't.

Corn kernels stuck in my teeth, I peel myself off the cushion and carry the bowl toward the kitchen, passing the massive bookcase that was a bitch and a half to build by myself. But I am woman, hear me curse like a mighty sailor (or however the saying goes) while I assembled that beast. It dominates an entire wall, floor to ceiling, and is lit with pink LED lights. My favorite books are on display, showcased by artfully arranged accent decor. It's the focal point of my home, and while the house isn't large, it's mine, and I'm damn proud of it.

Could I have bought a bigger house like those fancy ones across town? Sure. I could have even fought harder with Gram to get her out of the shack and into something a bit…upgraded. But in the end, I was happy with my cute, two-story contemporary off Main Street, and she was better off staying where she was.

Where the memory of her daughter is strong.

Between my divorce settlement and The Scorched Page, I do okay. And sure, I still live like I'm the little girl who ate pasta and butter for dinner four nights a week and hot dogs the other three because they're cheap and easy meals, and Gram was never the same since the accident that killed my parents. But I'm not hurting for money anymore, and now that my grandmother has arthritis in almost every joint in her frail body, I do what I can to help her, but she's stubborn as the day is long. She stays holed up in the shack by St. Crowe Lake, the one that's getting more difficult for me to upkeep by the day.

The more repairs we make, the more issues we need to repair.

It's an endless cycle, a money pit. But Millicent Benson was born in the home, and by God, she's determined to die in it.

No thanks. I prefer my little white house on Anne Avenue, with its spacious, white kitchen. The huge center island with its prep sink sold me on the place. I added three cushioned bar stools, where I eat most of my meals. I haven't used the dining room once since I've been here, with the lonely, six-seater, blackened-oak table the perfect spot for my mail before I sort it. But I had a hell of a good time picking out the furniture. I love the rustic pieces against white walls and espresso wood floors.

I got so used to adapting to Jason's style—cold and modern, hard lines—that I never realized I'm the opposite. Fluffy blankets, pinks, and everything girlie. Warmth. Inviting.

After depositing the bowl in the sink, I grab a glass of water before leaning against the cabinet. "I'm screwed," I say aloud. "Who the hell wants a twenty-eight-year-old divorced bookworm who fantasizes about fiction men?"

The only answer I get is the rain hitting the roof.

"Exactly!" I punctuate the word by holding up my glass. "No one."

I take a large gulp of water, my imagination running wild over Rhys Ravenstone. The app makers picked the perfect, over-the-top name for an antihero. And I sure had fun building my idea of the perfect man.

Six-five.

Artfully disheveled hair that's so dark it appears black.

Ebony eyes that are sharp enough to cut a man right to his soul.

Tattooed flesh stretched taut over thick cords of muscle.

Pierced penis, because why the hell not?

And a scar that cuts across his left—

"The hell?"

No, like, for real. It's midnight, and a nasty storm rolled down from the Appalachians. There's no reason on earth someone should be ringing my bell this time of night, especially since I don't have a single friend other than Brooklyn Ross. And she would never just show up at my house, not when a text would do instead. As for my family. It's only Gram and me...

Gram.

Oh, God.

On instinct, I grab two vital items. The first is my cell phone on the coffee table. The second is the baseball bat stashed in the coat closet near the front door. I dial 9-1-1 but don't hit Send. Without unlocking either the deadbolt or the knob, I shout, "Can I help you?"

"Charlotte Mallory?" The deep rumble on the other side of the locked door is *very* male and *very* irritated.

"Who's asking?"

"Are you Charlotte Mallory?" Each growled word is a bullet that seems to penetrate the Georgian Deco Fiberglass door. It came with the house, and I realize now it offers shocking little protection. If the enormous man on the other side of the smoked glass wants in, he's one hundred percent getting inside my home through this door or the many first-story windows.

Glancing at my cell makes me wonder if I should hit the Send button. My thumb is hovering. All I need to do is lower my finger a fraction of an inch to bring one of Sheriff Tom Whitcomb's deputies—if not *the* man himself—rushing over here.

Instead, I hesitate, shouting, "You're the one who knocked on this door, pal."

Why am I engaging with this man? It's nighttime. It's pouring. Stranger danger, for fuck's sake. He has no business darkening my doorstep, and in the beats of rain-soaked silence that follow, I can actually hear the whoosh of my blood and the hammering of my heart. The bat is growing heavy only because my hands are trembling, and I lower my arm before I drop the damn thing.

"Are you Charlotte Mallory?" He repeats the question slowly, each word clearly ground out between gritted teeth.

Daring to step closer to the door, I squint, trying to make out as much of him as possible. Thankfully, he's standing under the glow of the porch sconce, and *hot damn*. The man is massive. So tall that the top of his head reaches the upper edge of the doorframe. And wide. Shoulders that broad should be illegal. His hair is dark, the shaggy, wet strands hanging over his face. This man—this stranger—is definitely threatening, and when I back away from the door, I release a breath I've been holding.

"That depends on who's asking." God, how I hate the tremor in my voice. But honestly, how can I hide it?

I'm rightly terrified.

It looks like he tilts his head to face the sky. Maybe to face the light? I don't know for sure. But it feels like forever ticks by, and during those pregnant moments, I'm certain the smart course of action is to call 9-1-1 and rid my porch of this unwanted pest.

…and I'm about to do exactly that when Mr. Stranger Danger speaks again and drops one hell of a bomb on me, blowing my practical plan right out of the water.

"Rhys Ravenstone."

Fuck me.

THREE

Day One

"Ha, ha." I kick my fluffy-socked foot against the base of the door. "Not funny, asshole. So, what, the whole app thing is a goddamn joke? What's next, you steal my identity?"

I want to think I'm too smart to get internet scammed, but Jason's news blindsided me. Lonely as well, and… Wait. No way am I victim-blaming myself here. I'm not in the wrong. I wanted a momentary bit of harmless fun. It's this jerkoff's fault for exploiting a person's good intentions.

"This isn't a fucking joke, Charlotte." There's a beat of silence, one heavy moment before, "Open the door."

Oh, yeah, sure. Pardon me while I also grab my wallet and bank account information for him. I might throw in my social security number, too, for kicks.

"I'm calling the cops."

"No, you're not."

His audacity.

"Yes, I am!"

"You do realize I can see the outline of your body through the glass."

I glance at myself, at both lowered arms. One hand gripping the bat and the other holding my cell. But I snap my gaze back to him and wish the cool air the storm brought was to blame for the chill that slithers its way up my spine. It's not. Nope, the fault is solely because of the deep timbre of the man's voice. Thankfully, I don't have a total brain meltdown and drag the bat with me when I dash to the dining room window. The angle doesn't allow me a clear view of him, so I run back to the door, aggravated—and a tad disappointed.

"Move away from the door and go to the grass. *Now*." Listen to me, sounding authoritative. This time, there's not a tremor in my tone despite being absolutely rattled to the deepest depths of my soul.

Oh, my gawd, he acts like I told him to go play in traffic. He huffs and puffs, making a big production of stomping down the three steps of my little porch. I dash back to the dining room and shove aside the chocolate curtains. I wanted wooden statement blinds but remembered how they're nothing but dust collectors. Lydia 'The Twatasurus' Wembley has a small team of cleaners whose sole task is to upkeep the blinds that cover the billion windows of their summer homes—yes, plural.

They're *rich* rich.

But back to this guy marching his substantial self across my recently mowed lawn. The soaked man stops, slowly turns, and stretches his arms out wide. Holy hell, he's exquisite. With his head angled downward, he's staring at me through the wet ropes of his hair. The rain molded his black tank top to his torso, rendering it a second skin. Tattoos cover his arms from his neck to his fingers, and I ache to examine those black-and-gray designs up close and personal and…

…*Charly, get your mind out of your unused vagina.*

Clearly, it's been too long since I've gotten laid.

Also, it's been too long since I've seen a man this good-looking.

Try twenty-eight years, to be exact.

Never in my entire life have I ever laid eyes on a man like him. He's like a unicorn standing on my front lawn. And he's apparently looking for me because he thinks I built him on an app.

Okay, it's time to wake up now. This wacky dream got way too real for its own good.

"Done staring?" he shouts, and I can't help the heat that blooms up my neck and settles in my face. He stalks back to my front door. "Let me the fuck inside, Charlotte."

"I don't know you," I remind him as if that settles this entire matter.

He rakes his fingers through his hair, and I swear I can actually feel his frustration. "I don't know you, either. Now open the fucking door."

Not the greatest way to convince me he's not a threat.

"You have exactly ten seconds to get your stranger-danger ass off my property before I really do call the cops." I raise the cell phone. Shake it, hoping he sees it through the smoked glass. "One... Two... Three..."

He backs away.

"Four... Five..."

"Goodnight, Charlotte."

I lower my arm and stop counting as this lunatic (or scammer) claiming to be Rhys Ravenstone marches his fine ass off my porch. Wish I was glad he's leaving (although the view of his ass is spectacular), but I'm not. Actually, my stomach is tangled in a tight knot. My head aches, and while I should probably call the cops to be on the safe side, I don't. Instead, I clean up for the night. Check every window to ensure they're locked tight before I head upstairs to the bedroom.

I bring the bat with me.

This has to be a cruel, sick joke. Someone must either be laughing at my expense or... This makes zero sense. I built a man from scratch. *Scratch*. Put each component together from a series of random features. I could have made him short, blonde, and purple-eyed. I could have put him in a green hat, an orange shirt, and blue shorts. Instead, I selected a black tank top, jeans, and boots. Everything this man was wearing—down to the exact placement of his tattoos.

Perhaps it was makeup? Maybe stickers?

While I brush my teeth, I keep the bat and phone with me, then lay them next to me after I crawl into bed. I search The Book Boyfriends app but find nothing. No answers. Now that I've matched, I'm met with the ridiculous screen of our overlapped photos encircled by that big-ass heart. Tossing my phone, I press a finger to my temple. The migraine from before is threatening a violent return.

This is ridiculous.

Absurd.

It can't be.

Shit like this doesn't happen in real life.

"Fuck you, Cupid. You don't exist."

And neither does Rhys Ravenstone.

FOUR

For seven years, the Wembleys had my Sundays scheduled down to the minute. Church was promptly at ten, with a formal brunch directly after. I sat among them, judged, and always found lacking. I hated Sundays. They were the worst days. Now, I enjoy a nice and leisurely breakfast and lazy afternoons, but after last night's shitshow, I inch out of the house, wary that crazy fucker is lurking around.

Thankfully, it looks like the coast is clear.

No stranger danger hiding behind the bushes or poised to jump out at me from behind a tree. Tired, my eyeballs sizzle under the sun's glare thanks to strolling around the internet far longer than intended. I found nothing about The Book Boyfriends app. Then I tossed and turned for hours before finally falling asleep—only to have my dreams haunted by a dark-haired, tattooed love interest with a scar on his left cheek.

Dressed in my new Sunday best—charcoal cargo shorts and a billowy white top—I speed walk to my car, keys in hand and white purse dangling from the crook of my elbow. Winters are harsh here, but summers are lovely. Humid, sure, but not unbearably hot. Jason and I took one vacation, and that was for our honeymoon. We visited a tropical spot, some random island, and being away from the Appalachians taught me one thing: I'm a mountain girl through and through.

Roughed.

Built to last, as Gram likes to say.

Durable.

I'm not afraid of taking a tumble because I always pop right back up on my feet.

That's why I didn't crumble to dust after losing my parents and how I held Gram together when she began falling apart. Jason couldn't break me, nor could his family intimidate me—much to their frustration.

I'm like a weed. Even if buried in shit, I'll still thrive.

But today, I'm on high alert, and the first thing I do after sliding behind the wheel of my sensible silver Nissan Sentra is lock myself inside the vehicle. Then I connect my iPhone, and music blasts unapologetically from the speakers when I turn over the engine. I only lower the radio—slightly—finding it blasphemy to muffle Gayle's "abcdefu." Do I sing along badly on my way to Molly D's diner? Yes, I certainly do, and I even keep the windows lowered because it's seventy-eight degrees on this lovely late June morning, and I want the wind in my hair as I drive through town.

Harley Cove is a quintessential small town. General store. Family-owned gas station. One big-box store, and trust me, no one wanted it here initially because the older folks were afraid it would put the mom-and-pop shops out of business. It didn't, of course, and is now one of our major employers. Only one dental practice and one primary care facility for a population of roughly three thousand people. There's a hospital one town over in Glendale. But mostly, we're a self-contained, tiny haven of awesomeness where everyone knows everyone. It sucks that the Wembleys are such a large part of Harley Cove, but one takes the bad with the good, I guess.

The town sits in the shadow of the Appalachians, and on days like this, when the sky is so crisp a blue, I swear it's like being on the edge of Heaven itself. As I drive by the Sleep 'N Go Motel, I wonder where Mr. Stranger Danger disappeared to last night. Hopefully off a fucking cliff for scaring the bejesus out of me. Shame on a whole grown-ass man for participating in whatever cruel trick someone is trying to play on me. Well, the joke is on them because I'm not a fool. I won't play along.

Hangry, I pull into the graveled parking lot, having to circle nearly the entire area to find a spot. Unlike The Crystal Room on the north side, which welcomes a more…upscale…patronage, Molly D's is relaxed. Here's where the 'cool kids' come on a Sunday. I weave around dusty pickups and sedans that have seen better days, and as I enter the diner, more than one head turns my way. It's fine. Small town, remember? Folks are curious. I went from middle-class parents to dirt-poor grandmother to the wealthiest family in Harley Cove to a middle-class divorced hermit.

The frazzled hostess rushes over and grabs a menu from behind the counter. "Good morning, hon."

"Hey, Mandy." I eyeball the knot of gray hair piled atop her head. There's a pencil sticking out of it, and when she instructs me to follow her, I watch the towering hairdo bob and weave.

"Here you go." She places the menu on the freshly wiped table—it's still damp. "You doing okay?"

Frowning, I nod. "Sure, why wouldn't I be?" Her cringe says everything without saying a word. "Oh," I mutter. "So, I was actually the last to find out."

Mandy glances over her shoulder, eyeing the crowded diner of working-class Harley Covers who have thankfully returned to their food and conversations. Now it makes more sense, why the entire damn room was rubbernecked when I walked in. "You know how the Wembleys are, always running their mouths. Bragging about this and that. Especially Lydia. That woman told everyone her boy was finally getting hitched to the *right one*."

Ouch.

"It's all good. Really." With a shrug, I open the menu. "I couldn't be happier for them."

"That boy did you dirty."

I give her the fakest smile in the history of smiles. "No, Mandy, we grew apart."

The standard answer—the one I'm instructed to give—slips easily off my tongue. It's the one the Wembleys forced Jason to pay me a fortune to give people when asked why we divorced.

We grew apart.

Not *Jason is a disgusting cheater.*

"You can go around telling other people that load of horseshit, but I grew up with Lydia Wembley. I remember her when she was Lydia Postwhistle. Even back when we were kids, she was a narcissistic sociopath who wouldn't think twice about selling her own mother for a dime. That whole family is rotten right to the core. Lydia's boy is no different. He's cut from her cloth." She waves over a young woman with lovely red curls that are pulled back in a ponytail. "Ana's your server today." Then she leans in close. "Between us, I think it's shockingly disrespectful that Jason's marrying that woman, but I'll deny I ever said it."

I sputter out a laugh, saying, "You and me both, Mandy, and I promise you, I'll take this conversation to my grave."

"You do that." She pats my shoulder. "Oh, hon, you're priceless." Mandy steps aside so the server can approach the table. "Chin up, Charly. Karma has a way of biting people in the ass."

As Mandy strolls away, the server recites the diner's standard greeting. "Hi! My name is Ana, and I'll be your server this morning. Can I start you with something to drink, or are you ready to order?"

I ask for coffee and a glass of water, and after Ana leaves, I scan the menu. Do I feel a few lingering stares? Absolutely. Do I pay them any mind? Absolutely not. Until one bold bastard takes it upon himself to slide into my booth, sitting his ginormous self across from me.

Of all the fucking nerve.

I look up and…

…he has a scar that slashes across his left cheek below his eye. Exactly like the one I gave Rhys Ravenstone.

FIVE

Get hold of yourself, Charly.

Rhys Ravenstone is fictional. This man, who dares to instigate himself into my space, is *very* real, extremely gorgeous, and enormous. His clothes are dirty, and his midnight-brown hair is unkempt. But it's his eyes… Those ebony eyes slice me like twin razor blades. Without a doubt, he's the man from last night.

I slap the menu on the table. "Okay, enough," I hiss. "This shit wasn't funny last night, and it's even less amusing now."

Holy shit, his scowl is terrifying. "And I told you this isn't a fucking joke."

I drag in a deep breath, hoping to find my Zen. Yeah, no. If Zen is way over there, I'm *way* over here. We're a million miles apart.

"How about this?" I *shoo* him away with my hands. "Run along and kindly go take a flying leap off the tip of your own dick."

For a fraction of a second, his expression is hilarious. He seems to be mentally trying to figure out the mechanics of that, then shakes his head. "Physically impossible."

"Oh, my gawd, cut the shit. You're not Rhys Ravenstone. That person doesn't exist. He's make-believe. An avatar. A fictional book boyfriend I created as a joke because I was bored."

"Yet here I am." His voice is a tight, low rumble of thunder, his eyes harboring the coming storm.

I flatten my hands on the table and lean toward him. He smells like last night's rain, and there's a hint of a shadow darkening his jaw. Also, he looks exhausted, as if he hasn't slept. Why do I feel guilty for his lack of sleep? "You're a predator," I accuse in a nasty hiss. "I don't know how you did it or hacked the app, but I'm going to figure it out and expose you as the scammer you are. And when I do, you're going to be in trouble." I bang my fist on the table. "Big trouble."

"I'm quaking in my boots."

"Damn right, you are." I lunge forward and swipe a finger over the scar on his cheek. It's real. *Huh*. Scowling, I try to wipe off his tattoos. Keyword: *try*. They don't so much as smear. So, I pinch at them, trying to lift them if they're stickers or something. Turns out they're authentic as well.

Okay, I don't like this, not even a little.

The smug bastard leans back and folds his arms across his massive chest, a smirk on his gorgeous face. "Satisfied?"

Ana returns with my beverages. Her gaze instantly lands on Rhys. I'm tempted to remind her to lift her jaw off the ground, but I can't blame her. The man is truly a prime specimen of masculinity. Even tired, with raggedy hair and luggage under his eyes, he's the sort of man a woman wouldn't mind licking to claim as her own. Confronted by this...*antihero*...live and in the flesh confirms something I've wondered about since the day I picked up *Haunting Rapture* and fell in love with the main male character.

Authors are correct—a facial scar *does* add the perfect splash of yummy.

In fact, it's so nice I'd lick him twice.

Too bad Rhys is an asshole here to either make a fool out of me or scam me.

"Do we need another menu?" Ana asks.

I glare pointedly at Rhys. "Do we?"

He gives her a curt nod but says nothing.

"Guess that's a yes, please," I answer in his stead.

Her grin is radiant. "Awesome. Coffee? Juice? We have orange, apple, cranberry, grape. Would you like a water? I can add a lemon for you if you like." Will she offer to pick it fresh next?

Still, Rhys doesn't say a word. He's not looking at her, either. Nope, he's staring directly at me, and it's...unnerving.

"You can bring him a coffee and a water, please, same as me," I answer for him again.

"Sure, okay, and I'll bring that second menu quick as a wink."

His hands are fisted on the table, and I slap them with my menu. "Wow. Manners. Guess you left them home, huh?"

"Apparently."

"Brought the sarcasm, though."

"Never leave home without it."

"Speaking of…" I look at my menu without reading a word. "Where did you say that was, exactly?"

"Not Harley Cove."

"Apparently," I snap, with it my turn to be smug as I hold out my hand. "Let me see your driver's license."

Ha! Got him.

Rhys digs into his back pocket and produces a black wallet. He pulls out a license and hands it over. *Fuuuck.* There it is, plain as day, his photo wearing the clothes he has on now, with his information listed beside it.

Date of Birth: 06/28/1995

Name: Rhys Ravenstone.

Address: 704 Laroux Avenue, Harley Cove, Pennsylvania 18431

Expires: 06/29/2028

Issued: 06/28/2024

Sex: Male

Height: 6' 5"

Shaking my head, I read those lines three more times, focusing on the issue date—which is today. Then I sit there staring at his photo for way too long before dragging my gaze back to him. This is insane. Absolutely wild. And when I finally fling the license back at him, I whisper, "This can't be happening."

"Why not?"

"Because magic doesn't exist." And if it does, it doesn't happen to me.

Ana returns in record time with a menu, coffee, and water. "Here you go. I'll give you a few more minutes. If you need me, call out to me." She spins around on the heel of her sensible white shoes. "Um, maybe a little wave instead. It's loud in here."

She's still flustered. Again, can't blame her. Rhys is intimidating and stunning, and under different circumstances, I'd be a drooling mess because he *is* my ideal man. I created him, after all, from scratch.

Jesus Christ, this is absurd. Insane. Fucking wild…

And undeniably happening.

"I've got breakfast," I offer because the scent of last night's rain clinging to him is bothering me.

Rhys switches from relaxed to tense quick as a whip. It's like a strike of lightning down his spine, with his jaw setting and a little flex at the joint. And his eyes… My gawd, the edge in them is lethal. His pride is almost tangible when he grinds out, "Thank you."

I'm no expert in men, but it doesn't take a genius to know those two simple words of gratitude cost him much more than whatever I'll pay for this food. And when we place our order, I expect a man of his size to get a hungry-man-sized meal. Nope. Two eggs over, a side of bacon, and wheat toast (hold the butter).

I order the same, and we eat mostly in silence because he's not a talker. Only when I can't take the awkward silence one second longer do I break it with questions I might regret asking.

"So, tell me, Rhys Ravenstone, do you have a family? A job?"

"No family." He leans back and extends his tattooed arm across the back of the bench. One corner of his mouth tugs up in a mockery of a grin. "And you gave the job."

Assassin.

I squeeze my eyes closed for a hot second, my stomach doing a nauseating spin. When I pop my eyes open, I whisper, "But you never actually killed anyone."

Because he wasn't actually alive until yesterday—as preposterous as this entire situation is—which he confirms with a slow shake of his head.

"Not yet." Rhys taps his temple. "But the knowledge of how to end a life is here. And the will to carry out the deed is here." He taps his chest over his heart.

Jesus Christ.

And on that note...

It's time to go.

SIX

Great, now my sensible Sentra also smells like the remnants of last night's storm and outdoors...and *man*.

Not to be rude, but my companion will get rather ripe soon if he doesn't get friendly with soap and water. Currently, he's taking up a lot of space over there in his seat, sitting disturbingly still while switching from staring out the windshield to gazing out the passenger's window as if he's seeing everything for the first time. Which, I guess, if he's telling the truth, he is.

But that's preposterous.

So, why does it feel true?

Because it is, Charlotte.

A nagging voice in my mind is telling me to believe in the impossible. To take a ginormous mental leap, trust my gut, and believe magic...Cupid, whatever...is real.

Okay, sure. Let's pretend this dude is actually Rhys Ravenstone, my antihero. Let's also pretend that the little poem-thing that popped up on the app after we 'matched' is true. That would mean we have one week to fall in love. Seven days—as if instalove is as common as a cold. But say, remarkably, somehow, we fall instantly in love.

What then?

Do Rhys and I ride off into the proverbial sunset and live happily ever after?

Sounds like an outstanding fairytale.

Keyword: *fairytale*.

Life, however, doesn't work that way.

Hearts are fickle beasts, and the more likely outcome is that we don't fall in love in seven days—or ever. He could snore like a buzz saw or despise how I chew. He might have a wonky toe I just can't stand or halitosis. What if the gentleman prefers blondes? Or worse, God forbid, he's a DCU person to my MCU gal. There are a million perfectly reasonable and hilariously petty reasons why people don't mesh, and with a clock ticking...

I already know exactly how this will end.

I glance at my car companion and bite back a laugh at the way he's suddenly gripping the 'holy shit' bar. Seriously? Pardon me for being familiar with the twisty back roads of Wayne County. No need for me to do fifteen miles an hour on Penelope Road when I can go...faster. *Much* faster. I'm half-tempted to toss him into the rushing current while driving along the gloriously scenic and frigid Delaware River. Especially when he cuts his eyes at me, giving me a glare for taking a bend too quick for his liking.

Being malicious, I give the wheel a deliberate jerk to swish him around his seat. I ask, "Do you have somewhere you're staying? Somewhere I can drop you?"

Like in the fucking river?

"No."

Goddamnit. "Let me guess, no money either."

"No," he growls, and again, like when he thanked me for breakfast, I know it wasn't easy for him to admit that.

I want to lie and pretend Rhys Ravenstone isn't my responsibility. Because if he's telling the truth (and this *feels* weirdly right), I brought him here. This man is *my* antihero. He's the book boyfriend *I* built and who was sent by Cupid to *me*.

That does, in fact, make Rhys my responsibility.

Still…

I bang the heel of my left hand against the steering wheel. "Jesus Christ." I steal a glance at him to find him staring right back at me. "This is crazy. You can't be real." If a brain had actual gears, mine would be spinning wildly, grinding metal against metal. "I'm an actual person with actual feelings, you know. I'm giving you one last chance to come clean. Admit that this is a sick game you're playing. I'm asking you nicely, right now, to tell me the truth. I won't be mad. Swear to God. I'll even take you anywhere you want to go. Anywhere. No harm, no foul. Just please stop. This isn't funny."

There's a beat of tension between us, filled only with Benson Boone's "Beautiful Things." When Rhys reaches over to cover my hand with his, the heat of his palm rockets through my entire body. "Charlotte, pull this car over."

Confused and suspicious, I slide a glance at him, but only for a second because this road *is* winding, and I *am* going fast. "Why?"

He pulls his hand away. "Stop. The. Car."

"And I asked why?"

"Obviously, we need to talk."

I nod at him. "Talk."

Oh, my God, the hostility coming off him hits me like a hot wave. "Not while you're driving like a fucking madwoman."

"Fine," I snap, and when I spot an area to pull off onto, I park and kill the engine. "Now what?"

"We get out."

Rhys exits the Sentra, leaving me with no choice but to follow. Apparently, now we're hiking because off he goes on a goddamn adventure. I chase after him, catching up to his long-legged strides along the side of the road and over the guardrails, down the gradual descent toward the river.

"Where are we going?" I call from behind him.

"For a walk."

Wonder how hard Captain Obvious would hit the dirt if I nailed him behind his knees. You know, the bigger they are... "Why are we going for a walk?"

He releases a long and loud sigh as if my reasonable question bothers him. Then he stops and turns. "Because you need a walk, Charlotte."

Oh, do I? "Me, I need a walk," I repeat snottily.

"What part of that simple sentence did you not understand, or should I say it in crayon?"

"You're a dick," I snap.

Up goes that eyebrow. "I am what you made me."

Pursing my lips, I slam my hands on my hips and glare at the arrogant asshole. "What part of 'I'd love nothing more than to drop you off any-fucking-where and return to my normal life' do *you* not understand?"

"If that were true, I wouldn't be here." Rhys destroys the space between us, grips my chin with one hand, and fists my hair with the other. He blocks out everything, and even though the scents of old rain and outdoors cling to him, I could breathe this man in all day, every day, and never grow tired of his scent. And therein lies my problem. I should be offended that he would dare put his hands on me, but here I am, struggling not to melt into his touch. "And we both know it."

"You can't be Rhys Ravenstone," I rasp. "He's not real."

Sexy as hell, the tip of his tongue peeks out to slide across the seam of his lips. He steps closer. Close enough that our bodies touch. "Accept the truth, Charlotte."

My gaze flicks to the scar puckering his left cheek. "How did you get that?"

"You put it there."

"I didn't."

Without hesitation, he says, "Fine, you didn't."

"This is insane," I insist, then, "Please, just tell me the truth."

He drops his head until our lips almost brush. "You put it there, Charlotte Allison Mallory, the same way you gave me this hair and this face." He releases my hair to grab my hand, pressing my palm to his chest. "And this body." Pressing my hand against him, he slides it down, down, down, and I gasp against his mouth when we cup his heavy groin. "And the piercing to go with it. But I have one thing you didn't give me."

"What is it?" I breathe, mentally tripping over what I added to the Antihero avatar after I swiped right.

His malicious grin captivates me. Devastates me. "Free. Fucking. Will. I don't have to love you. I don't even have to *like* you." He brings his lips close to my ear, grazing the upper shell to send a riot of chills skidding across my fevered flesh. "Now, I shared my secret. I dare you to confess yours."

I want you to kiss me.

Of course, I don't admit this. "Last I checked, you aren't my priest," I retort with a dry laugh as I yank my hand away from his substantial...*member*.

"No, I'm your antihero, Charlotte. You made damn sure of that."

"Too bad I didn't make you my Houdini. At least then, you could have made yourself disappear."

Rhys's laughter is harsh as he shoves me away. "Clever, but you can't get rid of me." He strolls to the edge of the river, and I hate that I like how everything about him is massive and formidable. Powerful—but in a thrilling way. "You brought me here, Charlotte, now you're stuck with me for six and a half days."

I guess each hour counts when the days are limited.

Four and a half days with this gorgeous man. I'll think of it as a sort of staycation—only with a living, breathing book boyfriend.

Best part?

No strings attached.

"Okay, sure. Whatever. Fuck it." I hold out my hand for Rhys to shake. "Let's do this. Deal."

"Deal." Rhys's large hand engulfs mine. He pumps it once but doesn't let go. He tugs me forward, colliding our chests. His lips hover over mine as he growls, "You owe me an apology for making me sleep out in the rain like a fucking dog."

Then he seals our deal with a scorching kiss, one that leaves me breathless and spinning—and suddenly glad I downloaded that app.

SEVEN

"A six-foot-five antihero is showering in my bathroom."

This is the weirdest sentence I have ever spoken—and I do say this out loud. To no one. Needing to speak the words to my empty living room because it's absurd to whisper inside the privacy of my mind. I'm half-tempted to call my one friend, Brooklyn Ross, and tell her about Rhys, but honestly, I'm afraid she'll think I've gone insane. Could I blame her? Absolutely not. I'm living an impossible reality, and the best course of action is…

…to take no action.

Pretend Rhys is just some random new guy I met and leave it at that.

On the way back to my house after our 'talk' by the Delaware River, we stopped at Target to buy him clothes. Rhys shopping is my new favorite shitshow. It was the equivalent of watching an elephant figure skating. He hated everything that wasn't black or dark gray. The problem is that we're in a tiny town in the mountains, and pickings are slim.

Dude is here for a week.

Rule is that he gets what he gets and doesn't get upset.

Unfortunately, he didn't know the rule, and he got pissed. There I was, driving his grumpy ass to the mall over in Glendale. Upside? We found a cute little coffee shop. I sipped my new favorite drink, an espresso-something with mocha and oat milk.

Rhys woofed down two venti black coffees.

How he isn't still wired and bouncing off the walls is a mystery, but okay?

Now, he's upstairs washing his ass in my shower.

And what a fine ass it is. You can bounce a quarter off that thing. Great. Now, my brain is hyper-focused on his amazing body, and that sends me spiraling down a rabbit hole. I can't imagine it's common for a book boyfriend to pop out of an app. So, while Rhys is busy doing his thing in my bathroom, I'm here scrolling on my phone, doing a deeper dive on the internet—*not* thinking about the kiss by the river.

Nope, not at all.

Or the gigantic erection that bulged in his pants when he made me cup his crotch.

I'm absolutely not thinking about that as I scroll away on the internet, finding nothing about Cupid's The Book Boyfriends.

Defeated, I return to the app and more brick walls because most areas remain closed—

"Jesus *Christ*, Rhys!" I drop my legs off the coffee table and toss my phone. Squeezing my eyes closed, I slam a hand over them for good measure. "Is there something wrong with your clothes?"

Every nook and cranny of his phenomenally muscular physique is scorched into my brain, right down to his perfect pinkie toes. Oh, how I'd love to play Ferdinand Magellan and leisurely explore his body, examining each tattoo, planting a figurative flag on him to claim him as my own.

"I'm air-drying."

The rumble of his seductive baritone does things to me no man's voice has any business doing. "Go air-dry in your room."

My house has three bedrooms. I gave him one. He can damn well 'air-dry' his perfect ass in there. It's bad enough I'm going against sound logic by allowing a stranger in my home, but now he's walking around butt-ass naked. It's too much.

"Why would I do that when you're down here?"

"Because you're nude, Rhys," I point out matter-of-factly, as if my hormones haven't spiked so high I can launch an ovary out of my vagina like a cannonball.

"I ask again, why would I go upstairs when you're down here?"

Apparently, logic—or, rather, manners—is missing with this one.

"In the real world, there's a thing called decency. People don't prance around naked in front of each other."

"I'm not prancing, Charlotte, and you're not *people*. You're *person. My* person." Oh, gawd, I sense him get closer. His body heat radiates around me. Also, the way he rolls my name off his tongue… It's sublime. Sends a warm flood from my flushed cheeks right to the juncture of my thighs, instantly soaking my panties. His touch is achingly gentle when he curls his fingers around my wrists. "Look at me."

I shake my head. "Not until you put on some clothes."

"Charlotte, look at me." Again, I shake my head, but his gruff voice is a gentle coax when he says, "This won't work if you refuse to trust me."

Trust? That's a big ask.

But isn't he the one crouching in front of me, fully exposed and completely vulnerable?

And just like that, I get why he's naked. He's not 'air-drying.' He's not being sexual. Rhys Ravenstone bared himself to reduce his power. He made himself smaller the only way he can to make me larger. This beast of a man is on his knees, stripped raw at my feet.

I allow him to peel my hand away from my face, and when I crack open my eyes, all I see is him. Everywhere. Nothing else but him. His beautiful face. His large body. And those fathomless, dark eyes. That razored gaze slices through flesh and bone to cut right down to my soul. Unnerved, afraid he can read my thoughts as if they're etched across my flesh like the tattoos decorating his. I flick my eyes over his face, admiring his full, sensual lips. The subtle cleft of his chin is the ideal accent to a chiseled jawline. A noble Greek nose sits between sharp cheekbones. Mine may have been the finger that tapped on the app, but an artisan pieced the parts together. Created a masterpiece of flesh and bone.

"You can't be real," I whisper.

Rhys takes my right hand and presses it to his pec. His heart beats steadily against my palm. "Do I feel fake?"

With a slow shake of my head, I say, "No."

His lazy grin sends a silly little punch to my gut. "Because I'm alive, Charlotte."

I slide my palm along his smooth pec. Curl my fingers around his left shoulder, gripping him. Water droplets from his wet hair drip onto the top of my hand. "I still don't understand how you can be here. *Why* you're here. Why me?"

Rhys trails his knuckles down my cheek, and it's the most tender way a person has ever touched me. During the years Jason and I were married, he never—*ever*—caressed me. Rarely held my hand. Never hugged me. But this powerful man is touching me as if I'm delicate enough to shatter. And okay, I made him this way, but he said he has free will. He doesn't have to be here. Can leave any time he wants. He doesn't even have to like me.

So...

Why is he gentle? Why does he want to be here when he can leave, go anywhere, and explore this world for six days? "You're exactly the sort of person who deserves a little magic, Charlotte."

"And what sort of person am I?"

"The damaged," he says simply, adding, "the wronged and the wounded."

Well.

He certainly got that right.

Something about hearing it stated so bluntly...stings...and snaps me right out of the moment. "Please go put clothes on before you catch pneumonia."

July is two days away, and tonight, there's zero breeze blowing in through the open windows. It's stuffy and humid, and the last thing this man will catch is a chill. And even if he did, he'll be gone in a week, back inside the app or wherever.

But Rhys stands, and again, I squeeze my eyes closed, grimacing at the sight of his extremely well-endowed pierced penis—which is face-level to my eyeballs when he stretches to his full height.

"Your modesty is misplaced," he remarks, and I hear a definite note of amusement in his voice. Thankfully, though, he sounds like he's walking away. I dare to open one eye and see him heading toward the stairs. God, his ass is spectacular. "We only have seven days, and I plan on using every part of me to make every part of you feel good until our time together is over."

Oh, God…

I gape at him as he strolls up the stairs, falling back against the couch with a huff. My brain is screaming red flags. My body, however, is ready for a carnival because, holy shit, his promise woke up something dormant inside me. Actually, I think those parts of my anatomy were never awake. I actually need to press my thighs together to ease the pressure building between them and the empty ache skidding across my nerves tells me it's going to be a long night.

A *very* long and *very* uncomfortable night, with me painfully aware of the man directly across the hall in the guest bed—secretly wishing I had the balls to climb under those covers with him.

Who the hell am I right now?

Someone who built a man and apparently wished him into existence, that's who. I'd be a fool not to live each of these next days with him to their full advantage…

…starting tomorrow.

Because I talk a good game, but I'm a chickenshit at heart, and I've only had sex with one man, and I'm terrified and excited and…

…and I fall asleep with an anxious little flutter in my belly and a silly smile on my face because, for the first time in ages, I'm eager to find out what the morning will bring.

EIGHT

Day Two

The curious whispers start the second Rhys and I exit my car at the local Court of Food and Drink. Last night, we thankfully didn't cause a mini circus when we raced through Target. But we went after peak hours, so the store wasn't busy. Today is a whole different story. It's morning, and the supermarket is bustling. The lot is packed, and after we grab a cart from the nearest corral, we mind our own business as we beeline toward the automatic sliding front doors. Unfortunately, we only get midway toward our destination—with Rhys subtly having me walk on the 'inside' rather than the 'outside' where the cars are slowly driving by—when the lot practically crashes to a stop.

And I do mean *crash*.

Paula Olsen, the local busybody, damn near collides the nose of her silver BMW into the rear end of Mr. Jenks's red pickup the moment she spots Rhys. Fair. The man is a sight to see, bathed in sunlight, dressed head to foot in black, a gorgeous villain with a scowl on his handsome face as he takes in the tiny community of Harley Cove.

"I plan on using every part of me to make every part of you feel good until our time together is over."

I need to stop thinking of the promise he made last night—and it *was* a promise, no doubt about it. Every time I do, I need a cold shower and a change of panties.

The screech of tires and the expletives that follow have Rhys shoving me behind him, putting himself between me and danger. The thing is, there *is* no danger. It was Paula who nearly collided with Mr. Jenks's Dodge, and now he's spewing the vilest words at the completely unflustered woman.

"Good Lord, Tod, I didn't even hit you," Paula yells from the driver's window. "And with the language! Stick your head back inside your car and go home."

"You're a menace!"

"And you're a mean old buzzard."

With the crosswalk blocked, Rhys frowns at me in question. "Is this how everyone behaves here?"

"Not everyone, no, but enough do, unfortunately. People suck," I say with a resigned shrug.

Thankfully, the bullshit doesn't last long, and once it's over, Rhys snatches my hand and yanks me forward. He pushes the cart with one hand, keeping mine in his other as he strides forward, oblivious to the open stares as we enter the store. I don't hate how natural it is to be with this man, especially since there's an expiration date to our time together. But hey, it is what it is, and I stroll beside him with an arrogant smile on my face.

But the grin flies right off my face with the blast of frigid air from the cooling unit. I'm shocked it's not snowing in here. Rhys notices I'm shivering in the pretty yellow sundress. Of course, I paired it with my trusty Doc Martens. I wear these bad boys everywhere, and as we traipse through the bakery section, I rub my arms to generate extra warmth.

"It's not that cold, Charlotte."

I will never *not* get weird and melty over how Rhys rumbles my name. "You're, like, what, ten feet tall and protected by a thick layer of muscle? Of course you're not cold." I march ahead a few feet to the bagels, muttering, "I don't know why stores set their thermostats to Antarctic during summer. It makes shopping miserable."

I grab a few bagels and half a dozen donuts from the case. When I spin around to carry them back to the cart... *Jesus Christ*. I turned my back on him for a second. How in the world did I lose a whole grown-ass man?

Seriously? I look right and left. Lift onto my tiptoes as if an extra inch or two gives me a better vantage point. Yeah, no, that doesn't work. Clutching my baked goods, I search the area for Rhys. I follow the murmurs, the mini commotion coming from the female cashiers. That's how I know exactly where Rhys is before I see him.

Scowling, I practically run over to where he is by a novelty rack of I Love Harley Cove shirts. "What are you doing?" I hiss, keeping my voice low. "You shouldn't wander off until you know—"

"What size are you?" he asks without looking away from the shirts he's flipping through.

"Medium, why?"

He stops at an ugly navy sweatshirt that reads *I Heart Harley Cove*. He slides it off the hanger and hands it to me. "Put this on."

I back away a step. "Why?"

Up goes one infuriating brow. "Because you're cold."

If it weren't such a wonderfully thoughtful gesture, I'd take exception to his saying it like he's speaking to a child. A slow, wide smile stretches across my face as I accept the sweatshirt. He even helps me pull it on, lifting my hair from the neck hole before fluffing my brown curls.

"Better?"

Nodding, I say, "Much, thank you."

God, that tongue when it peeks out to wet those plush lips. It's criminal. "I'm glad."

And his gruff voice... It has a direct line from my ears to my vagina.

Speaking of voices... I cringe when Nancy O'Dell sidles beside me, her customary smirk in place. The baby-blue retro swing dress is lovely. The cream cashmere sweater draped around her slender shoulders makes her look like she stepped out of *Mad Men*. "And *who* is *this*, Charly?"

Newly divorced, she's devouring Rhys with her eyes, and I don't like it, not one bit. I have no right to be jealous, but here I am, practically bursting at the seams with possessiveness.

Rhys, however, glares at her like a roach that crawled across his boot. Before I answer, he wraps his big hand around mine and tugs me close to his side. "Hers."

Well, now.

He's summoned a storm of gossip that will rip its way through Harley Cove. Not that I give a shit. I've spent my life with my head down and my lips sealed. The girl who behaved. Who colored inside the lines and kept quiet when Jason fucked around. What I should have done rather than pretend I was the problem in our marriage was speak up for myself. Never allow the Wembleys to control my narrative. I should have been loud. Told people the truth, how Jason was relieved that I lost the baby, and how he'd built a whole life with Lisa behind my back. I should have told the truth about Harley Cove's golden boy, that he's nothing more than tarnished goods from a shitty family.

And that's why, barely holding in laughter, I say, "What he said." I point to Rhys. "He's mine."

Rhys yanks me away from Nancy to pull me down aisle five, forcing me to walk double speed to keep up with his quick strides thanks to his incredibly long legs. Finally releasing my laughter, I will never unsee Nancy's shocked expression.

Priceless.

Let them talk about me. Let them gossip. Let Nancy tell people how a gorgeous stranger arrogantly claimed he was mine—I dare her.

I glance behind me and laugh harder and louder when I see Nancy still by the rack of novelty shirts, gripping her cart, gaping at us as we walk away. Eventually, Rhys stops to grab a can of vegetables, examining it like he's reading *War and Peace*.

"Uh, Rhys." I tap him on the arm. He answers with a grunt. "While I appreciate your loyalty, and it was awesome to see Nancy stunned stupid, truly, you can't go around acting all caveman. We don't do that here."

Without taking his gaze off the can, he says, "Caveman would be tossing you over my shoulder and carrying you back to your house, stripping you out of that pretty dress, tossing you on the bed, and fucking you until you can't walk. That's caveman, Charlotte. Announcing that I'm yours is simply stating a fact."

Pardon me while I pick my jaw up off the floor. The most delectable vision of this gorgeous man, who oozes sex from every pore of his flawless body, hovering over me, fills my mind. For a second, I can't see anything else. Only him, doing exactly what he said. Tearing off my dress. Sliding off his black jeans and tank top. His hands roaming my body. Me exploring his tattooed, sun-kissed flesh. His pierced—

"Carrots or corn?"

"Porn?" I choke out, swinging around to see if anyone in our immediate vicinity heard him. "Why would you ask me if I want porn?"

"Corn, Charlotte." The can looks tiny in Rhys's tattooed hand when he holds it up to my flushed face. "*Corn*, with a *c*."

"Oh, carrots, please," I mutter like a complete idiot.

"Both it is," he announces with a smirk.

He takes off down the aisle, selecting items from the shelf, carefree abandon, and when we arrive at the meat section, I cringe because I can practically hear the call of the wild echo around him. Now, look, I may be frugal, but not with food. We all gotta eat, but goddamn, the prices have gone up to the point of crippling. I'm not hurting for money anymore, but I'll always be the little girl everyone made fun of for wearing rags to school and who survived on peanut butter and jelly sandwiches for lunch.

Rhys, however, has no concept of money. He grabs one of every package of red meat in the case. I'm right there to put most of them back. He can shove that scowl right up his perfect ass because there's no way I'm buying grass-fed Kobe beef, a prime rib big enough to feed an entire family. The man is out of his ever-loving mind.

"Nope, absolutely not, no," I insist, shaking my head.

"I need to eat," he grits out.

Not intimidated, I face him with arms crossed over my chest. "You don't need a trillion dollars' worth of meat."

If he keeps lifting his right eyebrow imperiously like that, I swear I'm going to shave it off while he sleeps. Either that, or I'll slap it clean off his beautiful face. "You're being dramatic."

"Dramatic? Really? Okay. I assume you can do fundamental math, right?" At his sour face over my sarcasm, I nod at the cart containing much of the meat I haven't put back yet. "Add up those prices, my dude."

He waits a hot minute before stalking over to the cart. Bent over, moving things around, he picks through the items, and when he's done, straightens and turns back to me. "How do you people survive here?"

"Barely."

He puts most of the meat back. "I'll do a job."

With a roll of my eyes, I lift on my tiptoes to say in his ear, "You can't exactly do a job search for 'assassin.'"

His hand lands on the small of my back, forcing me to suck in a breath at his touch. "You smell nice."

"So do you," I whisper.

"You tasted good when I kissed you."

I haven't been complimented much, but even if I had, that one is a doozy for sure. "Thank you."

Rhys leans away to search my face as if we're not standing in the butcher department surrounded by people who are openly gawking at us. "I'm going to kiss you again, Charlotte. Every-fucking-where."

Oh, God...

"Rhys."

I've read countless books where a male character's eyes darken. Never thought I'd see it in real life. *Wow.* Like, holy shit. Rhys's eyes are bedroom-y, hooded, grave. A mischievous grin tugs at his lips. "If we were alone right now, I'd tear you apart." I know I'm in trouble in the very best of ways.

Rhys pushes me away, and I swear to God, I feel the flush throughout every part of my body. Suddenly, my clothes are too close to my skin. I'm too empty. Hollow. I want to jump this man's bones right here against the meat refrigerator, and what's worse is that he knows it.

But what does the cruel bastard do now that he's got me all worked up?

He goes right on shopping like he didn't light my fuse just to watch it burn.

After causing quite the scandal, we head back to finish grabbing what we need, with me checking in with Brooklyn. Along with being my best—and only—friend, she also works at The Scorched Page. She's a lively twenty-six, hilarious, and, like me, loves everything about romance novels.

Everything at the shop is running smoothly, and everything between Rhys and me is going well. Until we get to the checkout line, and he notices the handsome male clerk looking at me a tad too long.

Fuck me.

"Eyeballs are a hell of a thing," Rhys says, too calmly, too conversationally, the words chillier than the air conditioning blasting throughout the store.

"Rhys," I warn.

The young guy flicks a nervous gaze from me to Rhys before suddenly finding our groceries far more interesting than our faces. His hands tremble as he grabs the items from the belt and quickly slides them across the scanner.

"All I'm saying is that it would be tragic if someone among the three of us, who aren't you or me, suffered a horrific accident that involved losing one—or both—of his eyeballs." Rhys glares at the poor clerk, who is damn near about to piss himself over the not-so-thinly veiled threat. "Stranger things have happened, Charlotte."

"Not here, they don't," I grind out through gritted teeth. "Bag the groceries, please," I say to Rhys to misdirect his attention. But he stands there staring at me like I spoke an alien language. In a huff, I grab one of the reusable bags from the bunch we brought in from the car before snatching up a bushel of fresh broccoli. As I toss the vegetables in the bag, I snap, "Holy shit, Rhys, like this. It's not rocket science."

He grabs a bag and begins loading it with groceries. "Do you often strive to make a person feel foolish when explaining a new task to them?"

If he pulled out a gun and shot me square in the chest, it'd hurt less than that admonishment. Because he's right, and I'm acting like an asshole toward him because I'm still riled over him getting me hot and bothered in the meat department. This man is...new. He was dropped into this world to live among *actual* human people. Being here must be a thousand times more of a shock to his system than his being here is to mine. At least I don't have to learn how to navigate everyday tasks people take for granted.

Like bagging groceries.

"No, I don't." I grab more items, helping him fill the bags. "Nor am I usually this snappy. I'm sorry." I motion with my eyes and a nod to the clerk, indicating Rhys should follow my lead and apologize to him.

He doesn't.

Fucking antiheroes and their arrogance.

NINE

"Remind me. This is what you call science fiction." Rhys points to the television where the Guardians of the Galaxy have recently escaped from Kyln. "Raccoons and trees can't actually speak."

"No." I pop the spoon out of my mouth. After swallowing the cookies-and-cream ice cream, I explain, "Technically, yes, this is science fiction, but specifically, it's Marvel. That also makes it a comic book movie, and that's a whole other thing entirely."

"Interesting," he says with a hint of a mischievous smile playing on his extremely kissable lips.

I narrow my eyes suspiciously. "But you knew that, didn't you?"

We're on opposite ends of the couch, our feet propped up on the coffee table, chilling, watching *Guardians of the Galaxy*

Vol. 1. I'm halfway through a pint of ice cream, and he's killing the bowl of popcorn on his lap (corn, with a *c*). There's nothing sluttier than a man in gray sweatpants and a white tank, and goddamn, he's fine as fuck wearing them. "Yes, Charlotte, I know animals can't speak."

I set my ice cream on the table before tossing a decorative pillow at him, not even caring that it knocks a bunch of popcorn out of the bowl. "No one likes a teaser."

"I would think that depends on who's doing the teasing." He throws the pillow back at me, hitting me square in the face. "And how you're being teased."

Okay, wow. Rhys pivoted this in a totally different direction—which explains why my mouth is suddenly dry and my vagina is wet when it's been the other way around for years.

"I see what you did there. The whole double entendre thing." I shoot him with finger guns because I'm not awkward at all. "Good one, dude."

The room feels intimate under only the glow of a lone lamp across the living room and the light from the television. The outside world seems eons away, leaving just the two of us. Movie night was his idea, possibly because I listed this as one of my ideal date preferences on The Book Boyfriends. I don't think either of us expected his inner movie buff to surface, but here we are.

I'm trying not to read too much into him falling wildly in love with Marvel (Drax the Destroyer is his favorite character), but after *Iron Man*, we skipped ahead to *Civil War*. He wanted more, so we jumped to *Guardians*.

Rhys is obviously hooked.

He also has a sense of humor. *Huh.* That's unexpected. A nice touch against the backdrop of that boatload of arrogance.

We pause the movie to collect the pieces of stray popcorn that flew out of the bowl, and while we do, I work up the courage to say, "May I ask you a question?"

"You can ask me anything, Charlotte."

Curiosity has been burning a hole in my brain. "How does this whole thing work? What are you, Rhys?"

"I don't understand the question."

"Yes, you do," I whisper.

He drops the last of the popcorn in the bowl before slicing me with those intense eyes. The muted lights play off the angles of his face, giving him a shadowy, almost otherworldly aura. "Am I a toy, a glorified robot? No, Charlotte. I'm my own person. You may have picked the parts that Frankensteined me together, but I'm not an extension of you."

"I see." I think for a long moment, chewing the inside of my cheek with the ice cream curdling in my stomach as I try to understand this insane situation Rhys and I are tangled in. "You have free will." At his curt nod, I press on. "You can leave anytime you want."

He nods to the front door. "I can walk right out."

I look down, staring at my hands folded on my lap. "Why don't you?"

"Why would I?"

"Why stay?" I ask with a shrug.

Rhys slides closer to me. The air seems to get sucked out of the room. "Because you're here, Charlotte."

"But you only have a few days. Why spend them with me?" I want to take back the reminder and keep him all to myself, but that's unfair. I was trapped in a miserable marriage, and although my cage was a fancy house in a gated community, it was still a prison. How dare I want to clip someone else's wings when they have every right to fly?

That would make me a monster.

Rhys grabs me by the shoulders and turns me, forcing me to face him. Then he puts a finger under my chin to lift my head. "Who is the man I need to kill who made you feel worthless?"

"It doesn't matter," I breathe. "*He* doesn't matter."

The trace of his knuckle down my cheek sends a wonderful little flutter in the pit of my stomach. "What a travesty it would be if I were to spend my days anywhere and with anyone other than you."

A whisper of a sigh leaves my lips, and breathless, I say, "For an antihero, you got a hellava way with words, Ravenstone. I don't remember adding poet to your profile."

"You didn't." Rhys leans forward, our lips nearly touching. "Sweetheart, that's all me." He takes my hand and brings it to his chest, pressing it over his heart so each hammering beat slams against my palm. "You lit the spark when you pieced me together, but I'm the fire"—he grabs my throat and tugs me to meet his mouth—"that's going to burn us both."

TEN

I had my first kiss at fifteen.
 Adam and I gave it our teenage best. Still, it was awkward and wet and weird, and I swore I'd never enjoy kissing—*ever*.

And I didn't for thirteen years. I tolerated it, sure. But enjoy it? *Meh*.

Not until this very moment.

I get it now. What the hubbub is all about. Rhys tastes delicious. Like popcorn and chocolate chips because that's what he was snacking on, but *everything* about him is… Yummy. I want to devour him and demand seconds. His lips are plush, his tongue exploring every inch of my mouth, and I swear to God, the way he's licking around in there has my toes curling inside my

favorite fluffy white socks. I have one hand twisting his shirt to haul him closer, close enough for his heat to seep through our shirts and flow into me. The other I bury in his hair to hold his head where I want, need it, while I kiss him back.

Who is this stranger I've become, this wild woman moaning into Rhys's mouth? This woman who yanks on his hair to pull a growl from him? I crawl onto Rhys's lap to push him back against the couch. Straddle him. Cup his face as I kiss him back with the ease and confidence of someone I barely recognize.

But I like her—this brazen new me.

I smile against Rhys's mouth when his hands land on my ass. He gives it a squeeze, followed by a playful smack. I yelp, then laugh, wiggling my hips over his swollen shaft straining in his sweatpants. I grind down harder, frisky as fuck, needing more contact.

Rhys wraps those muscular arms around me and keeps me there, taking control. Owning my mouth, my every whimper and gasp as he thrusts up, dry-pumping his cock across my aching pussy. Never in my adult life have I been this turned on. I rip my mouth from him and throw my head back on a desperate gasp, seeking air. But all I smell is him, that rich spice of his soap mixed with the warm scent of…him.

Intoxicating me.

He takes advantage of my exposed throat, nipping at the sensitive flesh, then licks away the sting. Sucks and kisses his way to my ear to whisper filthy promises of what he's going to do to me. And I want it all.

Everything.

All of him.

But I hesitate when he goes to lift off my shirt, the old insecure me rushing right back. "Let's get this off you."

"No, wait." I slap his hands away because there's only one who has seen me naked, and he obviously found me…less than desirable.

Rhys Ravenstone is flawless from head to foot. He deserves perfection in return. Not a woman who doesn't say no to a pint of ice cream. Jason's sort of emotional abuse left a scar even though Rhys doesn't seem to care that I'm carrying ten extra pounds—which isn't much, I know, yet each one hangs off me like an albatross.

"I warned you once, Charlotte. Modesty has no place between us." Rhys's tone may be ominous, but I can't stop the exhilaration that shoots through me as I lower my hands. Nothing heals a lifetime of rejection faster than that first moment of being accepted for who you are. "Good girl."

Oh, my fucking God.

Is it possible to actually see feminism sprout wings and flow out of a woman's body? Because I swear, I see mine flying off into the great unknown.

"Raise your arms." At Rhys's gruff command, I reach for the ceiling, and after he peels off my shirt, I'm straddling his lap in nothing but a white lace bra and grungy sweatpants…

…and he's studying me like the answers to the universe are written across my boobs.

Rhys skates his warm palm between my breasts and up my throat. Runs his thumb along my bottom lip. He dips that finger inside my mouth when my jaw goes slack, tracing the pad along my tongue. The hunger in his eyes sends a rush of heat straight to the juncture of my thighs, and when I roll my hips, his rumbling growl has me answering with a desperate moan.

The loss of his thumb leaves me oddly hollow, but he's quick to recapture my mouth with a kiss. But I need more. Much more. Every part of me is needy, empty, and wanting. It's like nothing I've experienced, and when he tears his lips from mine and instructs me to "hold on tight," I follow his instructions as he stands, carrying me toward the stairs with me locked around his waist.

Up we go, with Rhys heading toward my bedroom. He alternates between watching where he's going and placing sweet, little kisses on my nose, forehead, cheeks, and lips.

"We don't have to do this," I reluctantly remind him. "You're not obligated to have sex with me. It's not part of our deal."

His grip on me tightens as we reach the top landing. "You don't strike me as a stupid woman, Charlotte."

"I try not to be," I say with a little laugh.

Let's ignore the years I stayed married to a cheating asshole, shall we?

"Then don't say stupid things."

"Fine." I give him a quick kiss. "I was just trying to be nice, anyway. I want this to happen."

"Make no mistake, I'm going to fuck you." His promise shoots a delicious chill down my spine. "And I'm going to keep fucking you as many times as possible until I'm sent back to the void." He talks as he walks, stopping when we reach my bedroom door. "Any objections, now's the time to voice them. You won't get another chance."

I roll my lips between my teeth and shake my head. Then, "Nope, not a single one."

"Damn right you don't." He strides inside the room and literally tosses me on the bed. I release a squealing laugh as he turns on the lamp on the bedside table. When he sees me shimmy to the edge of the bed, I think he assumes I might try to run. "Stay," he snaps. "And don't you dare take off those clothes. You're mine to unwrap."

Like a gift.

But he's mine too, and when Rhys nears the bed, I hop onto my feet. "No fair. I'm the only one shirtless."

I remove Rhys's shirt, purposely skating my palms over the eight-pack abs. His body is magnificent, and when I finally reveal the glorious ink tattooed across his sun-kissed flesh, I trace my fingers along the gray-and-black skulls. "You're beautiful," I breathe.

Rhys wraps his arms around me. "You better like what you see." He kisses the top of my head. "You made it."

"No, all I did was pick a few things. It's like you said before. I may have Frankensteined you to get you here, but everything else, the things that actually matter... The rest is you, Rhys." I rest my chin on his chest and look up at his face. "I'm glad you're here."

I barely get those last words out before Rhys swoops me up and slams his mouth over mine in a punishing kiss. He uses his powerful body to move me backward until the backs of my legs hit the bed. I tumble onto the mattress and quickly pop up on my elbows. Rhys follows, climbing on top of me. With trembling hands, I explore his chest, marveling at the play of muscles beneath his taut and decorated flesh. Relishing the power caged inside him.

Rhys braces his weight on one arm, and I gasp when he cuffs my throat, restricting my air just enough to send a frisson of fear slithering through me. This is the part when I'm supposed to be all, *oooohh, a hand necklace!* But guess what? In real life, with Rhys...

Not gonna lie, it's a bit scary.

And I kinda like it—a lot.

"You may have brought me here, but who owns whom?" Rhys's growled demand comes with another squeeze around my throat. "Say it, Charlotte. Admit that while I'm here, you're mine." He lowers his head to lick the seam of my lips. "And I'm yours."

"Fine," I rasp out, desperate for air. "Sure. I'm yours."

He eases his hold, and I take a deep gulp of air. He grinds his length against me, letting me feel every achingly hard inch of him before he crawls down my body. "Lift your hips." I do as he demands as he shimmies my sweatpants over my ass and down my legs. When he traces a single finger along the waistband of my white lace panties, I press the back of my head against the pillow and squeeze my eyes shut. "No, I want them open. I want you watching me."

Fuuuck.

My eyes spring open, and my gaze locks on his. "I'm embarrassed," I admit.

"Of what? You're with me."

Oh, God, there's that lovely little flutter again. "I've been with one man, and he, um, he..." *Jesus, Charlotte, spit it out.* "We weren't... Um... He wasn't fond of my body. Actually, he hated everything about me."

Rhys keeps glancing from my face to my pussy, barely covered by the thin scrap of lace-covered cotton. When I'm done with my mortifying admission, he kisses my abdomen, right on the sensitive spot below my navel. "I'm not your ex, Charlotte." He brushes his lips a teeny bit lower. "And I'll tell you a secret." A third kiss, this one much lower. So low, he dips the band of my panties to press his lips against my fevered flesh, and I swear to God, I forget to breathe. "I've never done this at all, so what a pair we make."

I bolt upright and actually feel my jaw drop. "Sex?" I blurt out. "You never had sex?"

But of course he hasn't, and when he lifts that single brow, I flop back on the mattress. His baritone washes over me when he says, "Sex is difficult to do when you lack a body, no?"

Oh, my gawd.

Rhys Ravenstone, the Antihero, is a virgin.

ELEVEN

"Well, you kiss like a pro," I tell him.

"Glad you approve." His sarcasm is thick, and then he spreads my legs farther apart. My instinct is to slam them back shut, but I resist the urge. "Be a good girl and keep these open for me."

I can live a thousand lifetimes and never not get the warm and fuzzies hearing Rhys Ravenstone call me his good girl.

Fuuuck.

This is crazy-strange. I'm used to being the *giver*. Jason mouth-fucking me as quickly as possible so I can hurry and get my teeth brushed, then go about my business.

But Rhys flipped the roles…and he's not in *any* sort of rush.

Nope, the man is taking his sweet time drawing my panties down my legs. He kisses his way back up. Licking and nipping my inner thighs. Studies my reactions to everything he's doing to learn what I like, what I enjoy the most, and what I'm not quite into. But it's when he reaches the juncture of my thighs and pries my legs apart even more that I tense, and he has to coax me back to a relaxed state with more kisses. More teasing.

And more of his filthy promises.

Each one I'm confident this man will fulfill.

"You're so pretty, Charlotte." The awe in his tone is a punch to my heart. "All of you." He uses his thumbs to hold open my pussy, and normally I'd die of shame. Instead, I watch in wonder as he examines my body. Whimper in ecstasy as he licks me from ass to clit. "And fucking delicious."

Rhys keeps a firm hold on me, keeping me wide open as he tongue-fucks me. Dips in and out, with the steady rhythm bringing me close to the first orgasm I've ever had with something that's not my hand. I fist the bedding, needing to grip something, or else I'm positive I'll spiral right off into another dimension. I bury my other hand in his soft hair.

Almost as if on instinct, he drives a finger deep inside me, and when I arch my back, and my cry echoes around us, he teases my clit with the tip of his tongue. I nearly shatter, but somehow, Rhys holds me together, keeping me safe as he pushes me toward the edge of a cliff. When he grips my hip with one hand to hold me tight, pumping that wonderful finger in and out, his tongue doing magical things to me, I throw an arm over my face to hide my tears. But Rhys growls, "No," and I fling it wide, embarrassed at the rush of emotions flowing through me.

Lighting me as every muscle tightens almost to the point of pain. Nothing matters except the pleasure centered between my legs. It skids across my nerves until I can't even take my next breath. Until white sparks explode behind my squeezed eyelids as warm waves of electricity electrify me.

But all good things must end, and as the wave recedes, I drag in a deep breath and…

…giggle.

My eyes fly open, and I slap a hand over my mouth to stifle my laughter, but it's too late. Rhys heard. He wipes his face—and oh, my gawd, that's the hottest thing I've ever seen a man do—before resting his chin on his propped-up palm. "Something funny, Charlotte?"

I shake my head, but I'm still giggling. "Sorry." My apology is muffled. "I think this is aftershock."

"Ah," Rhys says as if he completely understands. "Remove your hand."

"Nope, I feel like an idiot."

"Charlotte," he growls. "Remove your fucking hand. I want to see your smile." I do as I'm told, and his expression softens. "And don't you fucking *dare* hide your laughter from me."

I nod. "Okay." As far as commands go, this one is…nice. Jason liked to say my smile reminded him of a cow. What a jerkoff. "Thank you for that." I nod at my vagina. "You're a natural."

Oh, Lordy, why is he frowning like I kicked his favorite puppy? "You don't thank me for giving you pleasure."

"Noted," I quip. Then, "Do me a favor?"

"Anything."

Wow, zero hesitation. "Please stand up." Before I'm even finished saying it, Rhys is off the bed and on his feet. "I want to take off the rest of your clothes."

He lifts a brow, watching me, not stopping me, while I remove his socks. He has nice feet. Not a wonky toe in sight. I unzip his jeans and shimmy them down his long legs, having to work them over the thick cords of muscle in his thighs and calves. And once he's naked, I step back and… Wow. Rhys Ravenstone is glorious. Truly stunning. Like a god that's come to life. All hard planes and angles, and sure, I went a tad overboard on the penis size. Do I regret my impulsive choice right about now?

Absolutely not.

Rhys is long and thick, and the glans ampallang piercing has me aching to learn what it'll feel like inside me. "Get on your knees, Charlotte." Oh, God… I hit the floor and wrap my fingers around his heavy shaft. He's warm velvet-covered steel, and when I pump my hand over him, he growls out my name. Empowered, more confident than I've ever felt in my life, I gather the pearls of pre-cum at the tip and use that wet to slick my slide back down, loving the way he throbs against my palm.

"Open your mouth."

Craving the taste of this man, for the drag of that barbell against my tongue, I open my jaw as he pushes forward. The blunt head of his cock rubs across my lips, once, twice, slightly salty and delicious. I open wider to welcome him inside, and when I do, I don't know whose moan is louder, his or mine.

Rhys keeps a firm grip on my neck as he drives into my mouth and as he pumps his hips to slide his cock across my tongue, my pussy clenching at the thought of the barbell inside me.

Wrapping my other arm around him, I use both hands to grip his ass. I take him as deep as I can before pulling away to tease him. To flick that piercing. Suck the head in a torturous tease. Lick my way down the shaft. Suck him deep. Drive him absolutely wild until he pushes me away with a growl.

I tumble onto the mattress, with Rhys climbing on top of me. He drags me up higher until my head is cushioned on a pillow. Poised above me, he slices into me with those abyssal eyes. "Why do I feel like I've waited my whole life for you?"

"Because you have." He takes hold of his shaft and positions himself at my entrance. "You sure?"

I nod once and wrap my arms around his torso, my legs gripped tight to his waist. "Yes."

Rhys enters me in one smooth slide, but he's big, and it's been a while. I can't fully take him, and when panic kicks in and I try to wiggle away, he holds me still. "Relax. Open for me, Charlotte."

I try, God, I try, but the stretch hurts. I slam my eyes shut as he keeps pushing forward, deeper into me. "Rhys."

He must hear the panic in my voice. "Look at me."

I shake my head.

"Charlotte, look at me."

I do, opening my eyes to see his beautiful face staring back at me.

"You're doing so good, sweetheart. I'm proud of you." He drives in farther and that barbell rubs along inside me. I gasp at the blunt glide. His grin is diabolical. "Lift your hips for me." When I do, he eases in farther. "That's it, Charlotte. Just like that. You're doing so well."

The slight shift of my body and the punch of his hips allows us to find our fit. Rhys swallows my cry, and with every deep, slow drive of his thick cock, he replaces the discomfort with a pleasure that brings me back to that precipice. This time, though, I'm not alone. He's here with me, and with each rock of his hips, he pushes us closer to the edge.

"You trust me." But his voice pulls me back, just for a moment.

"Yes," I rasp.

"I'll never hurt you."

"No," I say with a shake of my head.

"I need you to remember that."

Breathless, needy, grasping at his ass, I ask, "What? Why?"

"Because I'm about to fuck you like I'm your villain."

Oh, my God...

Rhys drives into me, hard, deep, growling in my ear. I score his back with my nails, crying out his name. Each brutal rock of his hips an exquisite destruction. He roars mine as I meet each thrust, lost in him. Never feeling more alive, more electrified, than I do with every merciless drag of his thick cock inside me. And then we're there...at the edge. Rhys sinks his teeth into the side of my neck, and I fall.

Oh, God, I fall.

But he falls with me.

We dive into the abyss, intertwined, splashing into an ocean of ecstasy. Drowning. Locked together. Lip to lip, gasping for breath, my exhale his next inhale. The flood of his orgasm mixes with mine until I don't know where I end and he begins.

Panting and sweaty, Rhys collapses on top of me. But he's a heavy fucker, and I tap him on the shoulder. "What?"

"I can't breathe."

"Oh." He rolls his big ass off me. "Sorry."

How is it possible that a man this formidable can be adorable. "Not a problem." I shove my sweaty hair away from my face. Normally, this is the part where I beeline for the shower, but I make no move to get out of bed. "That was... Wow."

"*Wow* good, or *wow* bad?"

Stunned, I turn my head to see Rhys staring at the ceiling, a frown marring his gorgeous face. His arms are folded behind his head, with his penis still semi-hard. But while he appears relaxed, he most certainly isn't. "Rhys, are you asking me if I enjoyed myself?"

After a tense pause, he grits out a terse, "Yes."

I flip to face him and prop up my head on my palm, struggling not to laugh. When I trace a finger down the center of his torso, he sucks in a sharp breath. "That was the best sex I've ever had."

The antihero that he is, he lifts that slightly cleft chin arrogantly. "Of course it was." He slides me some serious side-eye. "I wanted to hear you admit it."

"Of course you did." Silly man fishing for compliments. Tired, I drop my arm and let my head hit the pillow. Rhys remains on top of the blankets when I crawl under the covers. "You're not going to sleep?"

"First, you left me out in the rain. Then you put me in another room. I assume that's where I'm staying for the duration of my time here."

With a roll of my eyes, I pat the mattress. "Rhys, get under the damn covers."

It's the melodramatic sigh for the win as he gets himself comfortable on the other side of the bed. Fuck that. I shimmy all up in his business and hunker in, resting my head in the crook of his shoulder. I throw my arm across his chest, maybe liking it too much when he tugs me in closer.

He kisses the top of my head. "This is where you belonged the first two nights."

"I know," I whisper. Then, I say so softly, I wonder if he even hears me, "Rhys?"

He nestles me closer on an exhale. "What is it, Charlotte?"

"I don't do this. This isn't me."

His powerful body goes tense. "What isn't you?"

"This." I don't know why I need to explain myself, but I do. "I'm not the person who has sex with strangers."

He relaxes, his hand landing on my head to stroke my hair. "Why does this matter?"

"Most men care about a woman's body count."

He's quiet for a long time, and all I want is for the earth to open and swallow me whole. Finally, he asks, "How many men have you been with, Charlotte?"

"Two," I admit. "Counting you."

"I see," he practically hums before adding, "Charlotte?"

"Yes?"

He stops stroking my hair. "I'm not most men. It'll make our days together less stressful for you if you remember that." A lifetime of tension eases out of me from the unfair judgment the Wembleys have thrown my way for absolutely no damn reason. "Sleep well, Charlotte Mallory."

More relaxed than I've been in…ever, I close my eyes. "You as well, Rhys Ravenstone."

Never have I ever felt more protected, safer, and cherished than I do in this stranger's arms. And no, it's not because I

Frankensteined him. Rhys is his own person, he said so himself. He can get up and walk right out the front door. The Book Boyfriends brought us together. But like oil and water, if two people don't mix, well...

No harm, no foul.

But here we are, pairing like cookies and milk.

Um, wait, let's go with bullets and guns. I mean, come on. Rhys is the Antihero, not the Cinnamon Roll. I'll leave that type of book boyfriend for someone else. This one...

He's mine.

At least for the next few days.

TWELVE

Day Three

Sorry, no.

Morning sex is super romantic in movies and books, but in reality? Absolutely not. There's morning breath, and after Rhys and I crashed without showering last night… Let's just say I'm crusty. Yeah, no. Morning sex is out of the question without first making friends with toothpaste and soap. If this makes me a killjoy, oh well. But Rhys takes my rejection in stride—shockingly—and, with a playful slap on my ass, sends me on my way to the bathroom while he lingers in bed.

Okay, but this man is criminally hot as hell wrapped in my sheets, with his sleepy gaze following me as I hurry across the room to the en suite bathroom. And yay me for not wanting the floor to open and swallow me whole as I do the naked jog of shame with flaky sperm stuck to my thighs.

I brush my teeth, marveling at the well-pleased stranger staring back at me in the mirror. The sex-knot tangled in the back of my curly hair will be a bitch to brush out, but the memory of how I got it has me smiling, looking like a rabid dog with a mouthful of toothpaste. I trace a finger over the raw bite mark on my neck, a tingle in my belly over the thrill at how I enjoyed that pain while Rhys gave me so much pleasure.

Huh.

I would have never imagined I'd be *that* woman. I was someone resigned to a lifetime of boring vanilla sex. But look at me now. See what happens with a dash of spice?

While washing off last night's…sextivities…my mind wanders to what new adventures await over the next four days. Four days. Suddenly, that doesn't seem like such a long time. In fact, it's the blink of an eye, and…

…the toilet flushes, and a second later, I'm scalded when the water turns too hot. I leap out of the stream with a yelp. Pulling back the white shower curtain, I see Rhys facing the shower while brushing his teeth.

"Shower time is sacred," I announce.

The arrogant man simply shrugs. "You were taking too long," he says around the toothbrush.

"Was not." I disappear back behind the curtain to finish washing.

"Our time together is finite. Every moment is precious." He jerks open the curtain. "Now move so I can get in there with you."

Well, if he insists…

I step aside to give him room, but he's huge and takes up most of the space. Although I've already washed, Rhys re-scrubs me from hair to feet, taking his sweet-ass time, and my gawd, I've never been turned on by something as mundane as a shower. But his hands are big and soothing as they massage my scalp and slide over my body. He even gets on his knees when he cleans between my legs, being *painstakingly* there.

He stands and says, "Turn around, Charlotte."

At his gruff command, I do as he says, spinning and placing my hands on the white tile wall for support because my legs are jelly and they're having difficulty supporting my weight. He lifts my heavy hair and places it over my shoulder. Gets his hands good and soapy before stroking my back. He slides his palms along my spine. Down the cleft of my ass. Kneads. Drives me absolutely wild with his demanding caress.

Unable to take much more, I turn to face him, giving him the same torment he gave me. I soap my hands and trail them over each peak and valley of his incredible body. Across the wide breadth of his shoulders. Over his shredded torso. Relish the way his abs contract when I slide my palms over them. Stroke his massive length from root to tip, his hiss the finest music echoing around us, especially when I give the barbell a gentle tug.

"Fuuuck, Charlotte," he groans.

"You're exquisite," I whisper, teasing his shaft, loving the tortured expression contorting his gorgeous face. I rise on my tiptoes and kiss his scar. Kiss his chin. His lips. "Even if we had four hundred days, it wouldn't be enough."

What the hell?

Where'd that come from?

I'm the woman who wanted a good time, not a long time.

Rhys wraps his arms around me, hugging me so tightly the frantic slam of his heart beats against me. He holds me like this for only a moment, one quick squeeze before spinning to face the wall. "Brace yourself."

That's the only warning I get.

Rhys drives into me hard and fast, my gasp morphing into a cry as he rocks his hips against mine. This isn't like last night. This isn't sweet or tender. No, this is a quick and furious fuck, and I love it, every hot second as he pumps his pierced cock into me.

I reach around to grip his thigh to press him harder into me. Pushing back to meet each of his brutal thrusts. His groans, the way he rasps my name, and the hot and hard length of him push me to the peak he had me at yesterday. "Come with me," I breathe, slapping my palm against the tile. "Oh, God, Rhys, come with me."

"Tell me when you're there," he growls.

And I'm close. So fucking close. Almost there. The barbell tickles deep inside me with every drag of his cock, and when he pinches my nipple—hard—I arch my back, crying out at the intoxicating mix of pleasure and pain.

My muscles tighten almost to the point of agony as those wonderful white sparks of light explode behind my eyes. Every nerve ignites, and before I even realize what I'm doing, I chant, "Now, now, now."

First, the swell of Rhys's shaft as he reaches his orgasm fills me, stretches me a moment before the flood of hot wetness follows. I ride the wave of my climax as I drop my head against the tiles, with Rhys still pumping his hips as he drains himself into me, my name a hoarse cry ripping from his throat.

We stay like that for a long while, with the water falling over us like rain. My legs ache, and when Rhys twitches inside me, I smile. "You're incredible."

"We're good together." Rhys is breathless, pulling himself out of me.

Okay, but why am I suddenly…empty? "That we are, baby."

We wash again, quick this time. Then, get dressed, and after a bagel breakfast, I tell him I need to check on my grandmother. It's been a few days, and I hate not seeing Gram that long.

"You say this like you expect me to protest."

"With only four days together, I doubt you want to spend one of them at my grandmother's house," I tell him as I finish washing the dishes.

"Charlotte," he drawls, "I don't care if we shovel shit for the next four days, as long as we're shoveling it together."

Well, now. That's about the sweetest thing a man has ever said to me.

"How about we not do that?" I suggest. "But she lives on St. Crowe Lake. We can have a picnic."

"Sounds like a plan." He dries the last dish and puts it away. "If this grandmother of yours is anything like you, she and I will get along well."

I snort out a laugh. "Gram doesn't like anyone. Her body may be brittle, but her mind is sharp as a tack. Her insults can cut a person to ribbons with a surgeon's precision."

Rhys slaps a hand to his heart and inclines his head. "I have been warned."

THIRTEEN

"About time you came. I was getting worried, Muffin," Millicent 'Millie' Benson remarks the second Rhys and I enter the house. She's sitting up today, thank God, on the same old brown couch I slept on for most of my childhood. She stabs a bony finger at the cell phone on the snack tray crowded with medication bottles and a glass of water beside the couch. "You could have at least called."

"Because you would have answered if I had?"

Frowning, she flutters a hand over the phone. "I don't know how to use this fucking thing half the time. I think the damn thing is broken."

"It's not broken." I kiss her cheek. She's scary-thin. I lay a hand on her forehead. "You feeling okay today? No fever?"

"Stop fussing." Gram pushes my hand away. "I've never been better." With her glasses hanging on a strap around her neck, she places them on her nose, shoving them way up. "Not here two minutes and fussing already." She squints and blinks as she drags her critical glare over Rhys. "Who'd you bring with you, Muffin?" Then to Rhys, "You sure are a big one. Not from around here, are you?"

"No, he—"

"Wasn't talking to you," Gram snaps at me.

"No, ma'am, I'm not," Rhys answers.

Gram points to the old and faded floral chair. "Sit yourself down, boy." Then she mutters, "Standing way over there, making me strain my eyes." Louder, she says to me, "Charly, do me a favor. Get the two of you some lemonade. Nikki made some fresh this morning. She's a nice girl, that one. Swear, she must be a saint the way she puts up with my cantankerous ass."

Gram laughs at her own observation.

Rhys crosses the living room, and as I watch him go, I'm embarrassed how nothing has changed in this house since I lived here. All Gram has allowed me to do is repair damage as the shack deteriorated over the years. God knows I wanted to either move her out or redo the entire place, but Millie Benson is stubborn as hell. It's almost as if she's preserving this tiny corner of the world, leaving it exactly as her daughter lived in it. Which I understand, but also, it's been tragically unhealthy for her to have festered in her grief and sorrow all these years, and no matter what I tried to do, I couldn't pull her out.

"Who are you, boy? Where are you from? What are your intentions with my granddaughter? Swear to God, if you hurt her, I'll beat you half to death, see if I don't."

Well, she's still feisty. I'll give her that much.

Once upon a time, Millie was an active woman. She was a star athlete in high school. Even set a record for the fastest female in Wayne County, *and* she still holds the title to this day. Nothing stopped her or slowed her down—except the hit-and-run that killed her daughter and son-in-law.

It wasn't her fault someone ran a stop sign, clipping the tail of my parent's car. It sent them into a spin, ending when their car slammed into a tree, killing them on impact. It was a Friday, and they were on their way to get me from school. Gram surprised us with tickets to a Broadway musical (I don't even remember which one). Instead, a speeding driver took everything from us in the blink of an eye.

A part of Gram died that day as well. Her mind deteriorated and her body followed piece by piece, leaving her a broken shell of a woman who survives on a cocktail of medications to make it through the day.

I stowed my grief and raised myself while also caring for her. It was…a heavy burden…for a little kid to carry.

Her kitchen is tidy but ancient and microscopic, without an update or upgrade since the seventies. And while I grab two glasses and fill them with lemonade—Nikki may be Gram's nurse, but in actuality, the woman is much more—I listen as Rhys gives half-ass answers.

I return with the glasses, and our fingers brush when I hand one to Rhys.

"Thank you."

"You're welcome," I say a bit breathlessly. Then I sit beside Gram. "Stop badgering my friend."

"Friend, my ass," she mutters. "I'd bet a dollar to a donut that he's more than a friend."

I give her a playful tap on the top of her bony hand. "Don't be fresh."

Rhys sips his lemonade before setting his glass on the side table. He walks over to kneel in front of Gram. Eye level with her, he tilts his head, studying my withered grandmother with her ashen, wrinkled skin and body that can't weigh more than a hundred pounds soaking wet. Nikki comes daily, but she can only do so much. She's not a miracle worker. Once the blood clots formed, it became a battle against time. We're fighting the clots with blood thinners, but the medication created tiny tears that caused internal bleeding. She had reparative surgery, but it was only a temporary fix. By now, she's been in and out of the hospital enough times to see the writing on the wall. My grandmother is on a one-way path, and although I know where it leads, it doesn't mean I'm prepared to reach the end of it—even though Millie Benson sure as hell is.

Gram is done.

I'm not ready to be alone.

What a quandary.

"I like you," Rhys states.

Gram's smug expression is a riot. "I don't give a shit."

Rhys narrows his eyes on her. "I think you do."

"Yeah, why's that?"

"Because you're not as crotchety as you want people to think you are."

Gram purses her grooved lips and glares at Rhys for a long minute before snapping, "You got me figured out, don't you, boy?"

"Takes a stubborn soul to know a stubborn soul."

"Muffin, where'd you say you found this one?" she asks me without taking her eyes off Rhys.

"She built me on an app."

Rhys's honesty has me muttering an exasperated, "Seriously?"

"You didn't add 'liar' when you made me, Charlotte," he says smoothly.

"Noted for next time," I quip, and if looks could kill, I'd be dead on the spot from the glare he slides my way.

But Gram, bless her, breaks the tension between us when she nods slowly, purposefully. "Yep, I believe it." Then she turns to me. "Scar's a good touch, Muffin. He'd be too pretty without it." She asks Rhys, "So, you gonna tell me your name, or do I gotta guess it?"

"Rhys Ravenstone."

Gram bursts out laughing. "That fucking figures. I'm Millicent Benson. My friends call me Millie. *You* better call me Millie."

Rhys cracks a ghost of a grin. He grabs Gram's hands. "Millie, when did you last go outside?"

"Fucked if I know."

Panicking, I flick my gaze to the door and then back to Rhys. "She doesn't go outside. God forbid she falls, or—"

"Would you like to go outside, Millie?" he asks Gram, ignoring me.

"I thought you'd never ask."

I lunge to my feet, waving my hands wildly. "No, no, I don't think that is a good idea. She's sick. Rhys."

"My new friend and I will be fine." Rhys stretches to his full height. "Isn't that right, Millie?"

Gram gives a confident nod. "We surely will."

"Charlotte, why don't you grab Millie's socks and shoes?" He wraps his hands around her feet and gives them a playful wiggle. "Wouldn't want you to catch pneumonia."

Just like I said to him when he pranced around my living room naked.

I shake my head, muttering objections as I march into Gran's bedroom to grab socks and search her closet for shoes. Returning, I see those two, forehead to forehead, whispering, laughing—conspiring.

"Here." I hold out the items.

Rhys takes them and, with painstaking care, puts them on Gram's feet. Then he stands but hunches over, extending his arm. "Lean on me." He takes Gram's slight weight as she pushes to her feet. He's her support, holding her steady when she sways. Then he glares at me when I dive to interfere. But that ferocious scowl forces me to back the hell off. "You mentioned a picnic."

"For us, you and me. Gram can't—"

"Gram can't what? What can't Gram do?" My grandmother snaps. "I got this big bastard here to help me do any goddamn thing I want." She winks at Rhys. "That right?"

Rhys confirms this with a nod. "Correct." His smile is pure mischief, and I swear to God, my heart melts seeing how patient and kind he is with my frail grandmother—who kept herself a prisoner in her home for such a long time that it's become the norm.

"Fine." I jab a finger at him. "But if anything happens to her, I swear to God, I'll fucking kill you!" My threat has zero fire behind it because Rhys keeps a firm grip on my grandmother as he walks her toward the door.

"With the dramatics," Gram mutters. "I'm the only family Charly's got left," she explains. "She's overprotective."

"As she should be," Rhys says as they slowly tread across the living room.

I watch as they go with my heart so damn full it hurts.

"Roslyn went shopping," Gram calls out. "How about you fix us some sandwiches, Muffin?"

"Gram..." My tone is heavy with warning as I stand there, hands on hips, as she and Rhys walk out the door.

"Sandwiches," she snaps. "We'll meet you by the lake."

But I can't be pissy, honestly. It's awesome to see Gram out of bed, off that fucking couch, and walking. Sure, Rhys was struggling not to laugh at Gram barking orders at me, but it's all good. I'll take it. Anything to see Gram happy and moving and outside in the fresh air. I even have my AirPods in and sing along (off-key, of course) to Taylor Swift, as if this is the most normal day in the history of days.

Oddly, it's certainly one of the happiest I've had so far.

FOURTEEN

"You never said where you're from." Gram is sitting in a folding chair facing St. Crowe Lake. Summer is stunning here, on the outskirts of Harley Cove. Away from the main part of town. It's calm. Tranquil.

Home.

My best and most painful memories are here on the bank of this picturesque, rural lake. Everything is green and bloomed, and the afternoon sun gives the illusion of a million crystals glistening in the blue water. Rhys is beside Gram, staring out at the Appalachian Mountains that stretch across the horizon to scrape the clear sky, and it's wonderfully perfect—achingly perfect—I'm afraid to move, to breathe, lest it crumble to dust and blow away on the breeze.

But then Rhys speaks, and the moment stays, and I inhale the fragrant wildflowers that grow around the lake. "No, I didn't."

Seated cross-legged on a blanket behind them, I bite the inside of my cheek to keep from laughing. *Immovable force? Meet unstoppable object.* I imagine these two stubborn creatures are having a blast butting heads.

What a shame Rhys's time here is fleeting. What a damn shame.

"You gonna fucking tell me or not?"

Rhys grunts out a laugh. "I don't come from here, Millie." He crouches to get eye level with her, and I perk up when he points to the sky, adding, "See that?"

Gram nods. "The sky? Yeah, kinda can't miss it."

"No, Millie, beyond the stars and the universe."

It takes Gram a bit of effort to turn her body to face him, but she eventually does. When she places her tiny hand on his cheek, she asks, "Are you an alien, son?"

He circles her wrist. "No, I'm not an alien."

"Oh, thank the Lord," she huffs out. "I can handle a lot of strange shit, but I don't think I'm ready for an E.T." She gives him a peculiar look. "If you're no alien, then what the hell are you?"

"Rhys Ravenstone."

She nods as if his name explains everything when it explains exactly nothing. "What *were* you?"

Rhys stands and glances at the sky with a heavy shrug. "Stardust. Shadows. A jumble of thoughts." He glances at himself. "*This*, for now."

The turkey sandwich turns to sawdust in my stomach. "Whoa, wait a minute. Rewind."

Rhys turns to me. "Rewind to what, Charlotte?"

"To the jumble of thoughts, Rhys." I spin my index finger in a little circle. "You had a consciousness in the void?"

He lifts a single brow. "Am I not a living being?"

"Yes, but—"

"And I wouldn't have a consciousness why...?"

Jesus Christ, is he serious? That must have been pure torture, floating in that no*thingness, his mind active.* I shouldn't care. No, I should not. What he is, was, or will be...*after*...is none of my business. Except I do care—too much—and after I swallow the lump glued to the back of my throat, all I manage is a hoarse, "Rhys."

"It is what it is, Charlotte."

"It's not fair." I flick my frantic gaze to Gram, silently begging for her help, but she's nodding in the chair, this small exertion too much for her. "It's not fair," I repeat in a raw whisper.

He sits before me, blocking out everything else. "No, it's not. It's not fair that I was aware of every fucking second I spent caged in that goddamn void."

And that's what I see in his eyes. The abysmal darkness reflected in them. I see his prison, and for the first time since... Since I lost my parents, since I lost my baby, since Jason made a fool out of me, I feel a crack in the wall I built to protect my heart from hurt.

I'd keep Rhys here to prevent him from suffering the darkness if I could.

I scrub a hand over my face, wanting to wish away a lifetime of my pain and *lifetimes* of imprisonment for him.

"Stop," he demands gruffly.

"Stop what?"

"Whatever's going on inside your mind." He traces a finger along my forehead. "It's going to be okay, Charlotte."

"No, it's not." How can he ever speak such a lie? "I swiped right and made a giant mess, didn't I?"

He pulls my hands from my face. "We'll figure it out." He glances over his shoulder at Gram. "Let me get Millie inside."

I nod. "Rhys?" When he stands and goes to walk away, I leap to my feet and grab his arm. "I *am* sorry."

"For what?"

"For bringing you here."

His brows slam together. "You regret it?"

"No!" I rush out. "God, no. I'm sorry that I… complicated…things."

"Complicated?" His one-sided grin is devastating. "How the hell can you possibly think this has been a complication? Now that I've seen your face, I'll get to bring it back with me into the darkness. You, Charlotte, have been the most precious of gifts."

Gram was already asleep in the chair. With Rhys carrying her inside, I stayed by the lake, shoes off and toes in the cool water. I close my eyes and turn my face to the sun, letting the heat wrap around me as the brutal hammer of time slams against my brain.

I wish I can unhear how everything's changed for him now. Nothing can stop the inevitable. He's leaving. Cupid matched us, but as Rhys said, we have free will. Love, much like a fart, when forced, ends up shit.

Look what happened to Jason and me. His family forced our relationship between us, and it turned out to be a giant turd. The difference is that when we divorced, I moved into a cute house across town. When Rhys and I end, he'll be in a void and I'll be here, both of us alone and both of us miserable.

Apparently, Cupid is an asshole because instalove doesn't exist. He set us up for failure from the start.

"Fuck me," I breathe.

"You beg so pretty. Remind me to make you do it later."

Startled, I spin to see Rhys directly behind me. *Jesus Christ.* Did he switch on Stealth Mode? Sure, I made him an assassin, but my gawd. "Better make it good, then."

Rhys drags his gaze over me, from the top of my brown curls, over my body as if he's seeing right through my cream knit tank and jean shorts, down to my bare feet submerged in the water. "Trust and believe, I will." *Goddamn.* He nods at Gram's grungy yellow house and at the tranquil lake I adore. "You grew up here."

It's not a question. Still, I answer with a wistful, "Yes."

Rhys removes his shoes and rolls up the legs of his jeans to join me in the shallow water. With him beside me, his presence is oddly comforting. "You know everything about me."

"I know what I selected on the app." The brush of our hands is electric. "I don't know a thing about you beyond that, Rhys Ravenstone. Not the things that actually matter about a person."

Our hands touch again. This time, he locks our fingers together as if it's the most natural thing in the world. "Like?"

"I don't know your favorite color or food or if you prefer winter over summer. We already found out Marvel is your jam, which is a huge plus." I lift on my tiptoes to muss his hair. "Just because I picked dark hair over light and brown eyes over blue doesn't mean I know *you*, Rhys. It's like you said. Cupid gave you free will. No one controls you or dictates who you are but *you*."

But only for three more days, then—*poof*—he's gone, back to the void.

Lost forever.

Rhys turns and traces a knuckle along my jawline before tilting my head up. The touch of his lips is the sweetest kiss I've ever had. Not sexual. Not demanding. It's soft, not asking for a damn thing. Then he looks out over the lake with a slow and sexy grin tugging at his mouth. "Being here, seeing this place, I can almost imagine you as a carefree child splashing in this water."

"Sorry to burst your bubble, but I never played as a kid," I admit sadly.

"Not at all?" He sounds honestly baffled. "Don't all children play?"

"I didn't," I counter with a shrug.

Rhys snakes his arm around my waist and pulls me close. "Why not, Charlotte?"

"Because I was busy caring for Gram and mourning my parents."

"I see," he says.

But he doesn't see. I tear myself out of his embrace to pace in the water, my feet kicking up the sediment. "You don't understand. We were all we had. *I* was all *she* had. The car accident… It didn't just kill my parents. It took everything from us. It took everything from her because it was *her* idea for them to go to Manhattan to see that show. She couldn't have known that fucking driver would speed right through the stop sign. Nor could she have placed the tree in the exact spot for my parents' car to hit it. You said life's not fair, and it's not. That day, that was life not being fair. It was the universe lining up perfectly to kill both my parents, destroying my grandmother here." I tap my head, then my heart. "And here, leaving me alone to figure things out."

"How old were you when they died?"

"Seven," I spit out like poison.

"I'm sorry, Charlotte," Rhys says quietly and gruffly. "You carry a burden no one should have to suffer."

"Yeah, no shit," I agree with a bitter laugh.

He wraps me back up in his arms, and while my first instinct is to push away, I fall against him. Melt into him. I've had to be strong from the moment Sheriff Addison came to get me at school on that horrific day and brought me to the hospital. It was in second grade, and at first, I didn't understand what was happening. And even once I realized my parents were gone, I didn't cry then, not even when we put them in the ground. I couldn't shed a tear. Someone had to hold Gram together, someone had to be her glue, and that someone has been me for twenty-one years.

But now, in Rhys's arms, I squeeze my eyes close and let it drain out of me. The grief and pain flow from me in a rain of tears that spills down my face until there's no more left. I set it free to be carried away by the wind.

Wiping my eyes and nose, I lean away from Rhys, feeling epically foolish. "I'm sorry." I don't cry, I don't do this, this isn't me.

He smooths my hair away from my face. "For what?"

"You have your own problems, yet I'm crying all over you."

He traces a finger along my brow. "I'm with you, Charlotte. What problems can I possibly have?"

Perplexed, I gape at him stupidly before holding up three fingers. "Oh, I don't know, maybe because you have three days before you get sucked back into a void?" I flatten my palms on his chest and gaze at him with eyes that still sting with the aftermath of an ocean's worth of tears to whisper, "I hate that we don't have more time."

"How about we worry less about the number of days and focus more on living the fuck out of the time we have left with each other?"

My God, this man. If I could love someone, it would be him—and not because I Frankensteined him, but because he's him.

Beautiful, glorious, powerful, *him*.

I wrap my arms around Rhys's neck and give him what I know must be the most pathetic smile in the history of smiles. "Sounds like a plan, baby."

But the hammer slams again, reminding me that time is speeding us toward a brutal inevitability we can't ignore.

FIFTEEN

Day Four

It's one thing to *be* an antihero. It's another to understand what it means to be one.

Here we are, at The Scorched Page, with Rhys perched on the edge of the red wingback chair, his nose buried in a book. I pointed him in the right direction, but he picked *The Sexy Shifter Upstairs* by Mikki Saint Raven himself. Great choice. It's a fun book by one of my favorite authors, featuring a hot-as-hell antihero with a heart.

Wonder who that sounds like.

Heh.

We've been at the bookshop for nearly two hours. Rhys has already blazed past the first spicy scene and is on his second cup of coffee. Brooklyn stands half-draped across the counter, her chin on her palm, still ogling Rhys. She's been managing the shop while I've been...otherwise occupied, and while I'm super tempted to spill the beans about him, I don't. If anyone would believe me, though, it would be her. She swears she once saw a UFO. I secretly assumed she was out of her mind.

Now...?

With my gaze fixed on Rhys, I wonder if Brooklyn wasn't crazy after all.

The Scorched Page is feminine with a vintage edge. It's like stepping back into ye olde Victorian bookshop but with modern amenities. Thinking back to when Jason made a nuisance of himself by coming here, I recall what a square peg he seemed within these walls. Rhys, however, fits perfectly. A main male character who leapt off the page as he flips through the pages of the book, the living embodiment of power and formidability.

He's sitting with his legs crossed, one ankle resting on his thigh. Today, a gray tank top breaks up the black of his jeans and boots. He traces a finger over his scar before tapping his chin, a frown knitting his brows. Up goes the brow for a moment, and when he uncrosses his legs, he parts them, leans forward, resting his forearms on his thighs, not once tearing his rapt gaze off the page.

"Where did you say you met him?" Brooklyn whispers as if Rhys can't hear her in the small bookshop. Joshua Radin's melodic voice drifts out from the shop's sound system, but it's low enough that he can hear us talking.

"Tinder," I lie.

And yep, he may be busy reading, but he's definitely listening if the subtle tilt of his head in our direction and the hint of an amused grin are indicators of his eavesdropping.

Brooklyn pulls out her phone from her back pocket and immediately downloads the app. "If that's who's on there"—she points to Rhys—"I'm getting on there too because, come on, the pickings are slim as fuck around here."

"Yeah, no shit." But I'm quick to add, "Rhys is one in a million. A unicorn. You won't find another like him, trust me."

With a resigned sigh, Brooklyn sets down her phone. "Probably not." Then, with a nod and a wicked grin, she asks, "So, when's the wedding?"

My bark of laughter has Rhys winking at me in a way that curls my damn toes, reminding me of how it took forever to get out of the house this morning. Oh well. There are worse things than being with a man who enjoys worshiping every inch of your body.

But it's only temporary.

"Hate to be the party pooper, babe, but no wedding bells in the near future."

Or ever.

Those words, though, taste like shit as they fall from my mouth. Worse, Rhys slams the book closed, suddenly pissed. And I'm angry as well. Now we're both in a bad mood even though we both understood from the start this situation is for a good time, not a long time. We have an expiration date, and while it wasn't an issue before, it's bothering me today for some unfathomable reason.

"Shame," Brooklyn whispers. "If he were mine, I'd chain that man to me and never let him go."

The idea of never letting him go doesn't sound bad. In fact, it sounds downright fan-fucking-tastic.

With Brooklyn out grabbing lunch, I'm nose-deep in my laptop updating spreadsheets. I love my spreadsheets. Without them, my business would dissolve into pure chaos. But I'm startled when Rhys slams his book closed with a loud bang. It's the scowl twisting his gorgeous face that has me confused. "What's wrong?"

Rhys storms over, holding up the book. "This is what you wanted?"

"What? No!"

He tosses *The Hot Shifter Upstairs* on the counter. "No? Then why download the app? Why pick the antihero?"

"You're reading too much into it, literally," I say with a shrug and a half-hearted laugh.

And perhaps a tad too flippantly for Rhys's liking because he strides around the counter to grab me by the shoulders, shove me backward, and pin me to the wall. "Tell me, Charlotte? Why me?"

"I don't know." I attempt to push him away, but it's like trying to move a wall. "It's complicated."

He puts his face dangerously close to mine. "Uncomplicate it."

"I can't."

"You won't." The hard shake pulls a cry from me. "Because you don't fucking trust me."

"I do," I insist, but it's a lie. I don't trust *anyone*.

It's difficult to trust when you've been betrayed for years. Jason looked me dead in the eyes and told me he loved me *for years* while he was living a whole other life on the side. His shitty family knew what he was doing behind my back and covered for him, and after I found out, I had to bite my tongue and play nice. So, yeah, no. Sorry, not sorry for having serious trust issues.

But Rhys isn't Jason—and not solely because I 'built' him with loyalty as a personality component. After being with this man every moment of every day for nearly a week, I think even without me having given him that trait, he'd still have it.

Free will.

And he's fundamentally…better…than most.

He was kind toward Gram and gentle with me. With what I gave him, he could easily tip in the other direction—dangerous and arrogant. Instead, he's a good man.

"I wanted someone who could make me feel alive." The truth slips off my tongue.

Rhys kicks my legs open, fitting himself between them. Grinds his erection against me. Shifts his hold to grasp my throat, squeezing. "Do I make you feel alive, Charlotte?"

"Yes," I breathe.

He nips my lips, pulling a gasp from me, and I swear to God, it's as if every character in every book that sits on these shelves is watching us in rapt approval. "Beg me."

I snap my gaze to the front door, watching three women stroll past the shop, but Rhys bangs the wall directly beside my head. I jump, my attention right back on him. "Look at me, Charlotte, not them. I want to hear you beg."

"No," I grind out between gritted teeth. "I know what's in these books, the darker ones. That's not what I want. I won't beg a man for any-fucking-thing. Why, so you can have power over me? Make a fool out of me? No, I don't think so, pal. I was a joke to someone once. Never again."

Rhys *tsks* me with a slow and measured shake of his head. "There's a difference between making a fool out of you and having fun with you." He takes a slight step back, only enough to fit his hand between my legs to stroke my pussy. To tease my clit through my shorts, pulling a breathless moan from me. "Beg me, sweetheart."

With my eyes locked on his, I whimper a broken, "Please."

"Please what?" he snarls.

I drag in a hard breath, rocking my hips to meet the grind of his. "Please, Rhys, don't stop."

He tilts his head, hovering his lips over mine. "You were the last thing I imagined when I was rotting in that fucking darkness."

I bury my hands in his hair, fisting the soft strands, relishing his groan because, just as he's studied me, I've learned a thing or two about Rhys Ravenstone. He enjoys a tiny splash of pain with his pleasure. God, his eyes, the way he looks at me. If we had forever, it wouldn't be long enough for me to get used to being looked at like this—and a rush of fear follows in its wake.

The realization that I'm going to suffer once he's gone hits me like a tidal wave, and it takes everything I have not to shatter into a thousand pieces.

"I want…" I whisper brokenly, my sentence trailing off.

"Tell me." Rhys releases my throat and settles his hands on my waist, the heat of his hands radiating throughout my body. "What do you want, Charlotte?"

I spread my legs wider, giving him better access as he shoves aside my shorts and panties. He pushes two fingers inside me, and on a cry, I admit, "More time."

SIXTEEN

Day Five

Obviously, Cupid never materialized out of thin air to grant us more time. But we sure had a hell of a great night—which led to a wonderfully lazy morning. Now we're in the Sentra, windows down, an eighties freestyle song blasting on the radio, speeding toward Reece Park. I've never been to the famous amusement park but have always wanted to go. I mean, come *on*, it's home to the largest roller coaster in the Eastern United States. How can someone *not* want to ride that beast?

And after riding Rhys last night, apparently, I can handle anything,

I sing off-key—loudly—most of the way…and it's an hour-long drive, poor Rhys. It's a hoot when he jumps in once he gets a feel of the words. Next thing I know, he's disco-ing out to *Party Your Body* by Stevie B right along with me, and it's more fun in a car than I've had in my whole damn life. So much fun that I'm almost disappointed when the GPS instructs me to take the next exit because we've arrived at our destination.

But we *are* here, and… *Wow!* Reece Park is massive and marvelously imposing—everything I imagined and more. It's loud and crowded, especially since it's a holiday week. No big deal. We get swept up in the excitement, and sure, it's a slog through the slow-moving traffic of sweaty bodies, but that's part of the experience. So are the crazy-long lines. Thankfully, there are plenty of snacks to munch on while we wait.

I bombard Rhys with cotton candy and chocolate-covered pretzels. Because that's exactly what someone's stomach needs before boarding Armageddon. This ride is four hundred and fifty-eight feet of pure adrenaline. At max speed, it hits one hundred twenty-eight miles per hour and has a straight drop almost right out of the launch. I've heard the twists and turns have the power to churn even the sturdiest of bellies, so it'll be super fun to see how Rhys holds up.

Lord knows I've refrained from ingesting anything except water while we inch up the line toward the intimidating ride.

Heh.

With the sun a pressure beating down on us, Rhys nudges his hand against mine. Smiling, staring ahead at the horde of people in front of us, I bump back. Someone stinks of raw onions thanks to the heat, so I bump Rhys harder, and when he looks down at me, I pinch my nose, make a cringe-y expression, and wave a hand in front of my face. Frowning, he none-too-subtly sniffs his armpit. I roll my eyes, shaking my head as I mouth, *'Not you.'*

'Oh,' he mouths back. Then he sniffs me. "Not you, either," he announces.

Laughing, I seize the opportunity to kiss him. Then I grab him and haul him super close to whisper in his ear. "Of course, it's not me. I made good friends with my deodorant this morning."

I hear him sniff me again, loudly this time. "You actually smell like sunshine."

"Do I? And what does sunshine smell like?"

"You," he says gruffly, his breath tickling the sensitive shell of my ear. "Like you've been playing outside."

"Nice," I remark. "And I bet you taste like candy."

With the most arrogant, one-sided grin I've ever seen, he steps back and holds up the bag of pink cotton candy. There's only a tiny bit left. "We'll have to remember to buy more on our way out."

"That we surely do," I agree.

The line moves up, and as we step with it, a group of three rowdy twenty-something-year-old guys behind us get a tad too close for Rhys's liking. He turns and shoots them a warning glare they tragically ignore. Instead, they get louder. Wilder. Bothering two young girls behind them.

See, here's the problem. The air is too hot, and the crowd is thick with assholes. Thrown in the insanely long line and we have ourselves a breeding ground for trouble. Especially when one guy pulls out his phone and snaps a photo of a girl without her consent. She's rightly upset and demands he delete it. Laughing like the jerkoff he is, he refuses. Of course, his friends encourage him to keep behaving like an absolute dickhead. Everyone around us puts as much distance as they can from the three guys, but it's a tight space. There's nowhere anyone can go, and no one says anything to the rowdy group, probably hoping to remain off their radar.

A glance at Rhys tells me this is a powder keg of a situation. My antihero is not happy—at all. The scene from the *Chronicles of Riddick* flashes in my mind, where the titular character kills a man with a teacup. I can't help but think that if these idiots don't pipe the fuck down, Rhys is going to murder one—or possibly all of them—with the sticky cardboard cotton candy stick.

Damn, and this day was going so well.

Leave it to dudebros to ruin a good thing.

"You got a problem with me?"

Oh, no.

Dudebro #1 did not just ask Rhys Ravenstone that. Please tell me he's not that stupid.

"Yo, man, I asked you a fucking question."

He did.

I flick my gaze to Rhys from scrawny Dudebro #1, and the dichotomy of them is frighteningly hilarious. Rhys, dressed head to foot in black, looks like he can break this guy in half with one hand. Dudebro #1, with his long, shaggy blond hair and a sad, patchy goatee, is wearing the ugliest palm tree-printed surf shorts. They are barely even the same species.

"I heard you the first time," Rhys says smoothly. Way too calm.

"So why the hell didn't you answer me?" Dudebro #1's laugh is slightly nasal, sort of like Spicoli from *Fast Times at Ridgemont High*.

"Because I don't speak to the dead."

Oh, Fuuuck.

He jabs a thumb at Rhys. "Did you hear what this asshole said to me?"

Dudebro #2 nods, his buzzed brown hair not doing him any favors. He's showing off some seriously shitty tattoos by wearing that white wife beater and loudly tropical surf shorts. "Just 'cuz he's big, that don't make him tough."

"Big man gotta big mouth," Dudebro #3 chimes in as if he should add to this shitshow of a situation. What he should do is shut up. He's what, a buck ten soaking wet? And he's my height. He's rubbing his hands together and sucks his teeth before saying, "Three against one don't make for good odds, bud."

"Now, look, we're all just—"

"How about you mind your fucking business, Grandpa?" Dudebro #2 says to an older gentleman who tries to calm this escalating situation.

Subtly, Rhys pushes me behind him. *Far* behind him. He steps forward and, with a lightning swipe of his fist, knocks the phone out of Dudebro #1's hand. It hits the pavement, shattering on impact. "Consider your picture deleted," he says to the girl whose photo the jerkoff snapped without her consent.

"You're a dead man," Dudebro#1 threatens. Then he makes the colossal mistake of peering around Rhys to nod at me. "You and your fucking girl."

Oh, Jesus. Oh, good Lord in Heaven.

Bad move.

Bad, bad move.

There's a stillness to Rhys even as a commotion breaks out around us. Parents rush to get their children out of harm's way. I mean, shit, all we wanted to do was come to Reece Park to eat some crappy fried food and ride some roller coasters. Not end up in a fight with three little dickheads trying to be big, brave men.

Rhys, his dark eyes razor sharp and fixed on Dudebro #1, taps his chin. "You get one swing. Make it count because I'm going to damage you so badly, break you so completely, I will leave a scar on your soul that will last for eons. Do you understand? Do you understand the amount of pain I'm going to inflict on your body? You will never recover."

Okay, even I feel the need to pee a little.

The guy lets out a little laugh—a *nervous* little laugh. I can't say I blame him. "What, are you crazy or something?"

"Or something," Rhys replies, his voice lethally smooth.

"Do it," Dudebro #3 goads his friend. "Hit him."

But the guy shakes his head. "I'm not hitting him."

Dudebro #2 tugs on the guy's orange T-shirt, but he's staring at Rhys. "C'mon, let's go."

"Yo, man, we were just messing around." Dudebro #1 frowns as he backs away from Rhys. He even holds up his hands in surrender. "I don't want no trouble."

The line moves up, parting around us.

"Hit the fucker," Dudebro #3 shouts. "Don't be a pussy."

Dudebro #1 leaps aside. "You fucking hit him!"

"This ain't *my* fight." Dudebro #3 backs up. "You started it," he mutters.

"Yeah, that's what I thought," Dudebro #1 spits out. "But I'm the fucking pussy, right?"

"Fuck you!" Dudebro #3 snaps.

Dudebro #2 steps between his friends. "Let's go!"

"We good?" Dudebro #1 motions between himself and Rhys.

"Are we?" Rhys glances over his shoulder at me. At my nod, he looks back at the three assholes. "We're good." But he grabs the guy by the front of his shirt to haul him real close. "Leave the fucking park. I won't let you walk out if I see you again."

Rhys releases him with a solid shove that sends him on his ass. The guy scrambles to his feet, and the second he's up, he and #2 practically trip over themselves, running away. It's Dudebro #3 who moseys his ass off the line. Once they're out of sight, there's a collective sigh of relief, and although we lost our place, we make slow progress again, moving closer to the ride. I'm determined not to let those jerks ruin the rest of our day, and once we finally board Armageddon, I scream my head off when the car we're in hits that vertical drop. It feels like the skin is pulling clean off my skull as we zip along the track. With the wind in my hair and the sun on my face, I imagine this is the closest thing to flying without wings. Everything is perfect, the most thrilling forty-five seconds of my life—and I got to spend it with Rhys beside me.

There's not a person on this planet luckier than me right now.

Breathless as the car pulls into the station, I lean forward to peer around the metal harness banded around my torso. "Was it fun?"

Rhys leans forward as well, his expression chilling, and in his eyes, there is a raging storm. "I should have killed that bastard for threatening you."

"What? No!" I tighten my grip on the bars, shocked that he's still thinking about those idiots. "It's over, Rhys. Let it go."

His jaw is clenched so tightly that a muscle ticks, and his upper lip twitches. "You, of all people, know I can't."

Because he's an antihero, which means he's inherently built for conflict.

I glance at the young kid who runs the ride as he unlocks safety harnesses before I whisper to Rhys, "I'm sorry."

"Fuck it," he growls between clenched teeth. "It is what it is,"

I sink back in my seat, waiting for us to be released, and once we are, Rhys and I go on a few other rides, but we barely talk. He's distracted, scanning the park, searching for the guys from the line. Probably hoping to find them to finish what they started so he can appease the need to obliterate Dudebro #1 for doing what most assholes do—run their mouths talking stupid shit.

While I watch him grow more agitated by the second, I realize that what I absolutely love on the page doesn't translate well into real life. Not that I minded Rhys humbling the guy and breaking his phone. No, not at all. Dudebro #1 damn well deserved it, but what doesn't smoothly peel off the page is the turmoil raging inside Rhys. The battle within himself to take it further. His need to demolish all three of them. The struggle to oppress that instinct must be its own special torture.

The silent drive home is a brutal contrast to how we drove here. Even a cough is awkward. I hate this tension, hate how when *Unwritten* by Natasha Bedingfield comes on, I would normally sing alone, but now, I remain painfully quiet. Rhys just sits there, quiet and angry, watching the lush summer Pennsylvania landscape as it flies past his window.

I can almost hear his inner dialogue.

Hear his every furious thought.

After we shower, we crawl into bed, and I expect us to keep to opposite sides. He surprises the hell out of me when yanks me to the middle and fucks me slow and deep. Never breaking eye contact. Never saying a word. Just commands me, every part of me, his powerful body making mine feel so tiny and fragile beneath him. He's not rough, but he's far from gentle. And when I breathe his name like a prayer as I find my release, he roars mine, with today's frustration and tension draining from him in almost palpable electric waves.

Rhys collapses onto me, his breathing labored, and as I stroke his back, I smile into the darkness, content that no one else in all the world can give this man peace but me.

SEVENTEEN

Day Six

Not every day can be a wild ride on a speeding rollercoaster—or the shitshow that went with it. *Thank gawd.*

Today, it's all about hiking, something I haven't done in ages. Rhys and I got up and out of the house early, and after a quick breakfast at Molly Ds, we headed to Humility Trail. It's an easy path, a relaxed one, that cuts through the dense woods just outside Harley Cove. Leisurely. I've walked it a thousand times over the years, always alone. It's nice to have company this time.

No, it's nice to make the hour long trek with Rhys, specifically.

He's in a better mood this morning, leaving yesterday's frustration behind. The best part? The trail ends at one of the prettiest waterfalls in Pennsylvania. We began the trek quietly, walking with a bit of distance between us, but with each yard traveled, we moved inward toward each other. Talked a little more until we bump into each other now and then, and we're having a lively chat about why villains are better than heroes.

Obviously, we agree.

Rhys is simply curious why I like the monsters over the good guys.

"I can't help it if movies and books usually give the villains a better backstory," I tell him. "They make them...juicer. People you want to bite into." When I give him the old side-eye, I see he's giving *me* that infernal single lifted brow. "Come on, you know what I mean. The bad guys are fun. They're always the more interesting characters. They're tragic and beautiful and..." I let my sentence trail off as I leap over a big fallen branch. Then I shrug. "A villain will never let morality get in the way of love. He'll do anything for his women, even if it means burning the entire world to the ground. Now, a hero, he'll do the 'right' thing, the so-called moral thing, every time, even if it means sacrificing his lady love. And therein lies the hero's fatal design flaw. That's why most women will choose the villain over the hero every time, all the time."

"And that's why you wanted me."

Again, I shrug. "I don't expect you to choose me over everything or anything at all." When I glance at Rhys, I'm glad he's focused on the stunning scenery, not on me, because I'm sure my cheeks are flushed red. And it has nothing to do with the wet heat of the humid morning and everything to do with how he touches me and kisses me. "I never expected you to be real, remember? I thought the app was just a silly build-a-book-boyfriend thing. Something to pass the time because I was bored. I never expected you to show up knocking on my front door."

His voice is soft and warmer than the sun filtering through the thick canopy of trees when he asks, "Do you regret that I'm here?"

Rhys Ravenstone suddenly sounds like a man hankering for reassurance. How wild since he confidently struts around butt-ass naked with his big ol' pierced dick flapping in the breeze.

"No, Rhys, I don't regret you're here." With a sheepish grin, I give him a little hip check. "In fact, I'm glad I didn't choose anyone but you."

He's not grinning back. In fact, he looks deadly serious. "If I…" He pauses as if measuring his next words carefully. "If we had forever, I would never be your fucking hero."

Threading my fingers with his, I give his hand a squeeze. "I know."

"And not because you made me this way."

"I know that, too," I whisper, my voice so soft it nearly carries away on the breeze.

Rhys keeps a firm grip on my hand as we stroll along the path, passing trickling streams and stepping around dead branches. He helps me over more than a few big rocks that I definitely don't need help climbing, but I love it when he puts those powerful hands on me, so nope, there's no way I'm protesting his assistance. Whenever I see an animal, I point it out to him and quickly learn that the smaller the creature, the more he likes them.

Seems my giant man has a tender spot for tiny things.

No wonder why he likes me. The top of my head barely reaches his chin.

Eventually, the heat and humidity get to me, and I slow to a practical crawl. "Thirsty?"

"I could use a drink."

We're nearly at the waterfall, but dehydration is deadly. Resting under a tree, I cop a squat and pat the ground. "Sit."

Rhys, looking damn fine in gray swim shorts and a white tank (I forbade him to wear black today), shrugs off the backpack. He drops in front of me, steepling his legs and resting his arms on his knees. I dig out two water bottles and hand him one. I swear to God, water never tasted so good or felt so refreshing going down.

"Have you ever lived anywhere other than Harley Cove?"

I shake my head and gaze at the towering maples, oaks, beeches, and hickories. "Nope, never, and I've only been on one vacation, my honeymoon, right after Jason and I got married." Releasing a dreamy sigh, I collect a handful of leaves and let them drop back to the ground. "I honestly never could imagine living anywhere else. These mountains are home. I love the slow way of life, the people, and the beauty of the changing seasons. Everything. Maybe not the brutal winters so much, but I guess I got used to that little bit of bad that goes with all this splendor." I stretch my arms and gesture around us.

Rhys slowly drags his gaze from me to the forest, taking in the magnificence of the rich greens and browns surrounding us. He listens to the tranquil quiet, broken only by the rustling of leaves and the distant cry of a bird. "It is beautiful here, Charlotte."

I slap his hand. "Baby, you haven't seen anything yet. You just wait." I pop to my feet. "Come on. I'm going to show you Heaven."

Rhys mumbles something as he slides the backpack on, and although I'm not exactly sure what he said, it sounds suspiciously like, "You already have."

I don't know what's more glorious, Doyle Drop Waterfall or Rhys, shirtless, standing in the waist-high plunge pool. The shadowy rays of the filtered sunlight cast diamond-like sparkles across the calm, crystalline water, with the crashing water thunderous music that's grown as familiar to me as my favorite songs. I always came here when I was a teenager to get away from…everything. I'd sneak off and sit here and watch the falls for hours, mesmerized, the roar drowning out my turbulent thoughts. The beauty reminded me that the world isn't so ugly after all. But life (Jason) got in the way, and this is the first time I've been here in a decade.

And I get to enjoy my most private—and sacred—spot in all the world with Rhys.

Now that he's been here, I'll forever see him exactly as he is—standing with his back to me. Water glistens off his body like a million crystals, a work of art that has come to life.

And he's mine. Just for now, this man is mine.

But I'm also his, and when he spins, I suppress the gasp that catches in the back of my throat when he extends his tattooed hand toward me.

Wearing only a pink bikini, I step into the water. My feet sink into the soft bedrock as I meet Rhys in the pool's center. He immediately sweeps me into his embrace and kisses me softly, sweetly, before spinning me so that my back is against his chest. We're facing the furious falls, watching the plunge into the pool.

"You were right."

"About?" I ask without turning around.

"This is Heaven," Rhys murmurs in my ear, sending a delicious shiver through me that has nothing to do with the cool spray hitting us. "Thank you for bringing me here, Charlotte."

"It was my pleasure. Thank you for wanting to come." I exhale on a slow, sad sigh. "I wish I could freeze this day."

Because tomorrow is Rhys's last.

"So do I." His whispered admission is so heartbreaking, I don't know if the wetness on my face is from the waterfall or tears. But then he hugs me tighter, and there's an odd…wistfulness in his deep, velvety voice when he adds, "I like you, Charlotte Mallory, enough that I would choose you over everything and anything."

And I can confirm that it's one hundred percent my tears when I say, "I like you, too, Rhys Ravenstone."

Too much.

So much that after he's gone, I'm going to suffer the loss of him for the rest of my life.

EIGHTEEN

Day Seven

The people of Harley Cove do not fuck around when it comes to July Fourth.

They colored the town red, white, and blue, with practically everything draped in the American flag. Today, restaurants serve patriotic-themed menus as the annual parade makes its way down Main Street. A day-long party in Town Square will follow, ending long after the fireworks spectacular generously hosted by Court of Food and Drinks. But the barbeques won't start serving, and the band won't play until Mayor Bradford gives his usual speech in the raised gazebo with his adoring family seated front and center.

Harley Cove is quaint Americana at its finest.

I get why some people prefer city living, with its bustling streets that never sleep, but I can't imagine life anywhere else. Perhaps because I know nothing else. What I *do* know is that when my parents died, I found Harley Cove a comfort.

Even though it worked against me during—and after—my marriage.

There's good and bad in everything.

Today is good.

Watching Rhys devour his first chili dog while wearing a white I Heart Harley Cove tank top (payback's a bitch) is hilarious. We arrived early, staking a claim on the street in front of The Scorched Page to get a good view of the parade. I'm snapping a ton of photos for Gram, and when the veterans march by, Rhys stands taller, straighter, and clearly proud of our soldiers who have sacrificed much for our country. They're followed by the middle and high school bands, then the current Miss Harley Cove. And on and on it goes, and although I've never been one for parades, watching this one with Rhys, I'm like a little kid again. Makes this all new again, innocent. Harmless fun as I sip an iced coffee while he finishes the last bite of his chili dog.

What I love most is how he walks behind me to wrap those strong arms around my shoulders when he's done eating. He's a weighted blanket, making me feel secure among the crowd. It's a painfully natural and protective stance, like one a boyfriend would do, especially when he absently taps his fingers to the beat of the music. The kiss he places on the top of my head not only adds more cracks to the wall around my heart, but it shatters the foundation, threatening to topple the whole damn thing.

When I sway my hips to the music, Rhys gives a little grind of his erection against my ass. "Keep it up, and I guarantee you'll miss the end of this parade."

Giggling, I say, "Sorry. Didn't realize I was wiggling."

"Yes, you did." He gives my ass a playful slap. "You have a great ass," he whispers in my ear, sending a delicious chill down my spine.

Last night, we cuddled. No sex. We simply…snuggled. After decorating the bookshop's exterior for the holiday, we grabbed a quick dinner at Molly D's. Then we strolled around town, hand in hand, talking before we returned home, put on a movie, and chilled. Not two people desperate to cram in as much sex as possible before Cupid comes for Rhys, but like we were on an actual date.

And this morning, we woke before dawn. He wanted to watch the sunrise because today…

Today is full of Rhys's last—everythings.

I turn in his arms. "Having fun?"

"Yes."

"I'm glad." I give him a quick kiss. "Told you. Wait until tonight when the fireworks start. Oh, my God, it's—"

"Charly."

Whomp, whomp.

Wanting to gag, I roll my eyes and slam down on my heels at Jason's voice behind me. I resist the urge to retch and instead slap a fake smile on my face. How I hate this man's smug fucking face. "Hello, Jason."

The good-time killer.

Oh, great, Lisa is with them.

They look like they stepped out of a Fourth of July billboard. Her red, white, and blue sundress is about one star away from being a replica of Old Glory. And if that ponytail gets any tighter, her ears will meet at the back of her head. A curious glance at her belly tells me she can't be too far along because she's not showing, not even a little. Either that, or she's terrified of gaining even an ounce of baby weight, thanks to Jason being a stickler for skinnier women. Lord knows I damn near starved myself to make that jerkoff happy. But in her case, it's dangerous. Not saying that's what's happening. But it's possible, and if it is, she's a fool, and he's a bigger dickhead than I thought.

"Who's this?"

"He's none of your fucking business," I reply smoothly as I turn to Lisa. "Congratulations on the baby and the wedding. I wish you both the life you earned."

Snide? Maybe, to people with a guilty conscience.

"What's that supposed to mean?" Jason demands, proving my case, and oh, gawd, wrong tone to use with me right now.

Rhys Ravenstone—antihero assassin extraordinaire—comes to the forefront. Oh, Lordy, judging by his expression, Rhys seriously looks like he's going to murder Jason right here on Main Street, surrounded by hundreds of witnesses. He even shoves me behind him, putting himself between me and my ex as he gets all up in Jason's business, towering over him by a good five inches.

He rakes a disgusted glare over Jason as if my ex is a roach that needs to be squished beneath Rhys's boot. "Who are *you*?"

Jason puffs out his chest and notches his chin in self-importance. "Jason Wembley."

Rhys looks at me but jabs a thumb at Jason. "What the fuck is Jason Wembley?"

Oh, my gawd, it's nearly impossible not to laugh. "My ex-husband."

Rhys's eyes become a lethal storm as he slides that menacing gaze from me to Jason. "Right. The little creature who needs to make women small to make himself bigger." He *tsks*. "How underwhelming you are, Jason Weasley."

Lisa slaps a hand over her mouth to stifle a giggle, but quickly swallows it when Jason shoots her a glare, one that, a year ago, would destroy me. Now, he just looks like a silly man trying to appear powerful.

Newsflash, he's not.

"Wembley," Jason huffs. Then to me, "Charly, you better put a leash on your new friend before he—"

Oh, shit.

Rhys clamps a hand around Jason's arm, quickly shutting him up. For a second, I stand there, dumbfounded, as he drags him, literally kicking, toward The Scorched Page. Away from eyewitnesses. With everyone watching the parade and caught up in the excitement, no one realizes Rhys practically flings Jason inside the shop, with Lisa and me rushing after them.

"Don't hurt him!" she yells, but clamps her mouth closed at the blistering glare Rhys shoots her.

I grab her by the shoulders, putting my body between her and the men. "I got it. It's fine. No one is hurting anyone."

But I swing around right as Rhys twists his fists around Jason's perfectly starched salmon-colored button-down. My ex struggles in Rhys's hold, but he's no match for the bigger man's strength. "I'm actually glad we've had this chance to meet," Rhys remarks, as if he doesn't have Jason dangling in his hold like a rag doll. "See, I've been morbidly curious to meet the man who hurt Charlotte so badly she needed to bring me here."

"Brought you here?" Jason bounces his frantic gaze between Rhys and me. "What are you talking about?"

Rhys gives him a hard shake. "Don't worry about it. That's not the important part. The important part here is that you hurt her. See, the thing is, for right now, she's mine. This incredible, smart, funny, sarcastic, stubborn, beautiful woman is mine." Rhys lifts Jason off his feet and puts his face inches from his. "And you fuckin hurt her. Grave mistake, Weasley. I'd say it's a downright fatal error."

Jason peeks around Rhys's enormous body. "Charly! You're just going to let this…this *friend* of yours threaten me?"

I beam Jason a wide smile. "Sure am."

Because I don't think Rhys will actually hurt him. Okay, sure, he's the 'antihero,' and yes, I made him an assassin, but technically, he hasn't killed anyone. Also, this is the real world. Rhys surely understands we have rules. Laws. One can't go around murdering people willy-nilly.

"If you ever speak directly to her again, I swear on all that's unholy, I'll slit your throat and pull your tongue through the hole."

Or maybe he doesn't understand—or doesn't care because he'll be gone by dawn, and I'll be alone to deal with the aftermath.

"You're insane," Jason half breathes, half laughs. There's also a noticeable tremble in his voice. Don't blame him. If Rhys said that to me, I would legit shit myself.

"Insane? No. Loyal, protective, arrogant, and dangerous. Absolutely."

When Rhys pushes Jason to the nearest wall, I throw out my arm to catch Lisa when she tries to rush to intervene. The slam of Jason's body against the framed picture of Pygmalion and Galatea by Jean-Léon Gérôme shatters the glass.

"Sorry," Rhys snaps over his shoulder, but Lisa's scream drowns out his apology.

"Shut her the fuck up," Rhys growls. "Now."

"Lisa," Jason says, gasping, having had the wind knocked out of him. "Don't make it worse."

"Do something!" Lisa demands of me.

With a snort-laugh, I ask, "Why should I? He was a shitty husband who cheated on me with you." I poke her in her chest, and she takes a protective step back. "For six years. But I could have forgiven that if he had left me alone and gone to live his happy life with his side piece slash girlfriend. But nope, he's still up in my business being a fucking nuisance. And you want me to save him from the one person who has my back? Girl, you must be out of your mind." Then I say over my shoulder to Rhys, "Go ahead, baby. Have fun."

"No!" Lisa wails.

Rhys bangs Jason against the wall again, hard enough that even I flinch. "Men like you are an affront to humanity."

"No, wait. Stop. I'm sorry!" Jason yells. When Rhys switches up his hold and grabs Jason by the throat, my ex-husband fights like a caged animal to break free, but that five inches in height makes a difference—as does the massive contrast in muscle mass. "Charly, Jesus, come on. I'm sorry," he pants out when he can't overpower him.

With a *tsk*, Rhys says, "I warned you."

Jason, a coward at heart, squeezes his eyes shut. "It was an accident."

Rhys leans away to glance with disgust at Jason's crotch. "Like the way you just pissed yourself?"

Wait, what?

I step to the side to get a better view, and yep… There it is—a dark stain spreading across Jason's pants. Giggling, I smirk. "Not such a big man now, are you?" And while his fight and humility shouldn't fill me with such satisfaction, it does. If anyone deserves to be brought low, it's this jerkoff.

Rhys takes Jason down with him when he crouches for a piece of the broken glass shattered at their feet. My stomach does a worried flip as I watch him drag my ex back up along the wall and press the edge of the glass to his throat, heedless that he's cutting his own palm. The jagged glass opens a tiny, shallow wound on Jason's throat, and although I've fantasized about this moment, about Jason getting his comeuppance for being an abominable dickhead, I don't want Rhys's last day to be this.

Messy.

Bloody.

Violent.

Also, Jason was a bad husband, true, but that's not a death-sentence-worth offense. Get the shit scared out of him, sure. But I don't want his death on my conscience, for what…? For wounding my pride and self-esteem? Even if Jason were dead at my feet, it wouldn't magically heal me. I have to do that work myself, one difficult day at a time.

"Please don't hurt me. I'm going to be a father."

Rhys digs the glass deeper. "Where was this concern when your child was inside Charlotte?"

The question guts me in too many ways. Let's go back to when I was a terrified eighteen-year-old who everyone saw as the girl from the wrong side of the tracks who nabbed herself the winning lottery ticket when she got knocked up by Harley Cove's golden boy. Of course, that wasn't exactly how it happened. Who cares about the truth when gossip is more fun to believe? By the time I miscarried, we were already married, and I had dropped out of college.

I also realized one vital fact that made Jason despise me—I'm not, nor could I ever be, a fucking Wembley.

Most folks in Harley Cove, including me, grew up feeling inferior to that family because they live in the biggest house in the nicest part of town and have the most zeros in their bank accounts. But the longer I spent on the inside, the more I realized their money can't buy them decency or integrity.

Lisa's weeping behind me, and while a part of me feels terrible that she's upset—the woman is pregnant, after all—this had to happen. This dam had to break, eventually. Things couldn't keep going as they were, with Jason quietly tormenting me as if he had every right to, simply because I'd been his wife.

"We were young," Jason rasps brokenly, sobbing. "I should have been better, and I'm sorry. Charly, I'm so sorry."

"Of course you are, *now*," I counter with a bitter bite in my tone. "When your back is literally against a wall." I nod at Rhys.

"And you're up against someone you can't intimidate and who for damn sure won't tolerate you bullying me."

"Let him try it," Rhys mutters. He throws the glass at Jason's feet and backs up to stand beside me, lending me his strength and power without doing anything other than taking my hand in his. "I'll fucking skin him and hang him on a meat hook."

And this is exactly why I wanted an antihero. I may have made Rhys Ravenstone an assassin, but the man isn't a cold-blooded killer. He could have beaten Jason to death or murdered him in a hundred different ways. He did neither. But he could have—*would* have—for me because antiheroes love getting their hands bloody doing the bad things moral men won't. More importantly, they light the match for their queen to set fire to the world.

What they don't do is whine like a little bitch.

"What do you want from me?" he whimpers with a stomp of his foot like he's a goddamn toddler. "More money? Done. I'll double your alimony. A bigger house? I'll build you the biggest house in Harley Cove. I'll even build one for your grandmother." He flicks his gaze to Rhys. "Now, call off your dog, Charly."

Before I can tell Jason to shove all that up his flat ass, Rhys smacks him across the face. Not a punch. Not a manly hit. Nope. A bitch-slap that leaves my ex with a giant red handprint on his cheek.

I'm sorry, but I have to laugh at Jason's shocked expression. Lisa doesn't help curb my amusement when she throws herself in front of him to protect her man like a human shield. "For the love of God, move."

"No!" she cries. "Don't hit him, please. He can't take it. You'll kill him!" she pleads with Rhys.

Jason wraps his arms around her waist, holding her in place, and I gape in astonishment at how cowardly he is—although I honestly shouldn't be surprised. He's spent his life hiding behind his parents. Stands to reason he'll hide behind his pregnant fiancée.

Rhys snorts with disgust. "You make me fucking sick."

"You?" I snort out. I jab my thumb at him. "I was actually married to this joke. Gross." I fake a disgusted shiver as I make like I'm gagging. "Tell you what, Jason, let's call it even."

"What?" he asks, peeking over Lisa's head. "What do you mean?"

"This." I gesture at myself before waving my hand at him. "This awesome moment of humiliation." I wink at Rhys and flash him an appreciative grin. "We're even. I walked away from you with a chip on my shoulder and trust issues, and you leave here today with a bruised ego. Deal?"

It's a fair bargain.

I get closure because seeing Jason piss himself was… *chef's kiss*

Lisa turns and glances at Jason's wet crotch before taking the tiniest step backward. Then she cups his face. "Walk away, Jason." When she spins back around, she strides over to me, chin up, and looks me directly in the eyes. "Women should protect women. I didn't do that. I owe you an apology, but not today because you won't accept it. But I owe you one, Charly. I know I do."

"It's whatever," I say, but it's not whatever, and while we may not have been friends prior to her becoming Jason's side piece, we were friendly. She backstabbed me, which hurt almost as much as Jason's betrayal. Like they were laughing at me, and when I nod at Jason, I say to him, "At least she's not a total piece of shit. You, though…" I pull my hand free of Rhys and march up to Jason. "This never happened. Do you understand? You and Lisa enjoyed the parade today, that's all. If you even *think* of causing trouble, you better remember that I spent ten years as a Wembley insider. I learned all your family's dirty little secrets." I love the sickened shade of ash he turns when I tap my ear. "You don't think I listened over the years? Let's talk for a second about all the conversations I heard with your father bragging about how he robs from his own company and how he hides the money from the IRS. Or how your mother skims from her charities to line the Wembley pockets. That's *some* of what I heard. Don't think I won't air your family's filthy laundry out all over Harley Cove." I leap forward and jab a finger against his chest. "Fucking try me, asshole, I dare you."

But Jason is already shaking his head. He glances frantically at Rhys, then Lisa, before finally back to me. "This never happened."

"Damn right it didn't." And damn, it feels good to threaten him. Smugly, I fold my arms across my chest and notch my chin. "Now, get the hell out of here. I'm done looking at you."

"Come on, Jason." Lisa grabs Jason's hand and pries him away from the wall.

Wobbly and trembling, Jason totters away. He keeps glancing over his shoulder as Lisa tugs him toward the door. But I put them out of my mind the moment they're gone. I sweep the past behind me and settle my hands on Rhys's hips, staring at his face. I wish to God—to Cupid—that this man was my future.

"Thank you," I whisper.

"For what?"

"Defending me."

"Someone needed to."

He's wrong. No one needed to defend me, and no one had until today—until him. "Actually, thank you for everything. For being nice to Gram, for the incredible sex, and for…everything. For being you. Thank you for an amazing seven days."

He kisses the top of my head. "Thank you for downloading the app."

When I look up at him, Rhys brushes his lips over mine. Nothing about him is possessive. Nothing is demanding. And when he pulls away from me, I want to drag him back into my arms and hold him forever, but I don't, and by the time we finish cleaning the broken glass, the parade is over. Rhys and I head back to Gram's house, to St. Crowe Lake, where we'll have a prime—and uncrowded—spot to watch the fireworks.

But as I teach Rhys the wonders of grilling and we enjoy a traditional Fourth of July barbeque with Gram, everything is moving in fast-forward. The day is speeding toward midnight, and no matter how loud I scream for it—beg for it—to slow, I feel each second bang against my heart.

The clock…

It keeps ticking.

And my heart…

I feel the first crack as it begins to break.

NINETEEN

I've always loved summer.

A July baby, I was destined to love slow, sun-kissed days that bleed into humid nights. Hazy golden dawns and flaming sunsets over the Appalachians make a person feel as if they can reach up and scrape their fingertips along the edge of Heaven itself. As if, when I close my eyes and listen real hard, I'll hear the voices of the angels whispering in the warm breezes that blow down from those majestic mountains.

As a kid, I'd come to St. Crowe Lake and sit for hours, pretending my parents were alive and daydreaming about tomorrows that looked nothing like the way my life actually turned out. On my birthdays, I'd stare at the night sky and wish upon every star to ease the loneliness and stop the hurt, but the universe never granted me my request.

Until I swiped right on an app that brought Rhys Ravenstone knocking on my door.

While most people are gathered in Town Square, I have the best seat in Harley Cove. Nestled between Rhys's legs, I'm wrapped in his arms on the bank of St. Crowe Lake. The upbeat thrum of "Cupid" by Sam Cooke (ha, ha, funny, you evil cherub) drifts out from the Spotify app on my phone. Gram is asleep, leaving us to watch the fireworks alone in our private little corner of the world. He's playing with my hair, gently tugging random curls just to watch them spring back into shape.

This afternoon feels like a lifetime ago.

"Your hair is so soft, like silken threads."

Instinctively, I go to smooth the riotous curls, but he blocks me. "I've always hated it. I wanted straight hair."

"Blasphemy!" he teases. "Your curls are pretty. Don't ever change them."

"I won't. Promise."

Rhys kisses my hair. "That's my good girl."

I exhale on a suddenly sad sigh, with time finite, sliding past us like the strands of my hair through Rhys's fingers. Locked on a single bright star, I'm like a little girl all over again. I wish. I wish, wish, and wish for something I have no business requesting because I'm asking for the impossible. For something I don't dare say aloud.

Something impossible.

It's not that I can't love Rhys Ravenstone.

I'm *afraid* to love him.

Oh, God, I'm so afraid.

This is reality. People rarely get their happily ever after. If one were even possible for me, I wouldn't have time ticking like a hammer against my skull. A brutal reminder that Rhys and I have only three hours left.

"Where are you, Charlotte?"

"Huh?" I semi-twist in Rhys's arms to meet his searching eyes over my shoulder. "Here, with you?" I tell him with a little laugh. "Where does it look like I am?"

"Your body's here, but your mind went somewhere else."

I turn back around and hunker in closer to him, relishing his heat against my back. "All of me is here, baby. Promise."

Baby? And it's not the first time I've called him this.

Who even am I right now?

"Don't drift away from me, Charlotte." Rhys's lips brush my neck, giving me chills, when he whispers, "Or you'll force me to find creative ways to keep you right here where I need you."

"Oh, really?" I breathe, suddenly hot and bothered, despite the chill coming in off the lake. "And how would you do that?"

"Hmm..." Rhys's hum vibrates through me, the sound slithering down my ear to skate across my nerves. He unlocks his hands from where they're entwined near my collarbone to glide over my breasts, teasing my nipples through my red T-shirt. "I think I can find a few interesting ways to hold your attention. In fact..." He lifts the bottom hem of the shirt, trailing his fingers along my abdomen. "I've thought of nothing else since you defeated your nemesis."

Defeated my nemesis?

Wow, that's one way of viewing this afternoon's…event. Not how *I'd* regard it, but okay, sure. Let's go with it if it keeps Rhys's hand on my body. "You helped," I remind Rhys because I must give credit where it's due.

He kisses my temple. My ear. My throat. He rearranges how he's holding me, moving his arm to slide his hand lower. Parting my thighs, I suck in a breath when he shoves aside my shorts and panties to slide the tip of his finger up and down my slit. A slow tease that has me lifting my ass, chasing his fingertip. "It was my pleasure, Charlotte."

How he purrs my name… It's the sexiest sound I've ever heard in my entire life. I lay my head back on his chest, a moan whispering from me as I reach between my legs to press his hand harder against me, needing more. More of his touch. Of the delicious friction. More of *him*. "Please," I rasp, my plea floating away on the breeze.

"Please, what, Charlotte? What do you want?"

To freeze time.

To stay exactly like this, with you, forever.

What comes out of my mouth is something else, something cowardly. A broken and desperate, "You."

"You have me." The 'for tonight' hangs unspoken between us, even when he presses the pad of his finger over my clit but doesn't move it. Simply holds it still, a light pressure, until I'm damn near about to scream with frustration. "I want the words, sweetheart, or this is all you get."

"You're fucking evil," I grind out.

"That I am." Rhys grabs me by the wrist and pulls my hand away, pinning it to the blanket. I slap my other hand over his.

"Move it or I'll stop." His breath tickles my ear when he adds, "Your words, Charlotte, use them."

Embarrassed, I lick my lips, mustering a whole heap of courage. "Please, Rhys, put your fingers inside me."

The second the demand leaves my mouth, those long, thick fingers fill me. They're a slow slide in and out that brings me to a fever pitch. "Like this, Charlotte?"

I nod. "Yes," I say breathlessly. "Just like that." He keeps up the pace, finger-fucking me as the first rocket explodes in the sky, lighting the night in a riot of red and gold. "More. Faster."

Rhys does as I ask, driving in harder, deeper, quicker. Still, it's not enough, and as the sky glows in a rainbow of sparks, I pull his hand away. I turn and pop up onto my knees. Then glance around to make certain we're alone. Of course we are. Gram's house sits on a quiet stretch of the lake. No one comes out here, especially tonight when most folks are at Town Square.

My fingers fumble as I unzip Rhys's jeans. I'm all thumbs as I shimmy them down his legs and pull out his heavy cock. I stroke him from base to tip, tugging on the barbell, pulling the most delectable moans from him as fireworks explode overhead. And when he removes my clothes and settles between my legs, sliding into me with a single punch of his hips, I gasp, having him inside a perfect *fit* as the stunning light show above us fades to black.

I hold Rhys tight, holding on to him with both hands. I whisper incoherent wishes. Broken pleas. I'm begging for things I have no business wanting, with the fragmented remains of the wall I built to protect my heart at Rhys's feet.

And in his hands is my heart, raw and aching and bleeding.

TWENTY

"Stay," I whisper. "Please."

Rhys releases a slow sigh as he strokes my back. "Can we not do this, Charlotte?"

"Why not?" We're in bed, spending our last moments in each other's arms.

The clock is ticking toward midnight.

I'm scared—terrified, actually. It's almost as if time is a weight pulling us beneath violent waves in a turbulent sea.

"Close your eyes and try to go to sleep. It'll be better for both of us that way."

"No." I sit up, dragging the blanket with me to cover my bare breasts. "I want you to stay."

For once, Rhys's smile isn't arrogant or wicked. It's achingly sad. "I can't."

"Why not?" I demand again.

"Do you love me?"

His whispered question cuts me sharper than any blade. "Do you love me?"

Rhys sits up slowly, his movements measured, the flood of moonlight casting his face in a pale glow. "If I say yes, you won't believe me. You'll think it's Cupid's work or because you pieced me together, and therefore, I'm compelled to love you despite my free will." He trails a knuckle down my cheek. "If I say I don't, will that be a lie? Either way, my answer won't be good enough. So, I ask you again, do you love me, Charlotte Allison Mallory?"

Do I?

I—

"Your hesitation says everything."

My eyes drift closed as my head tilts down, my heart and head locked in a violent battle. Is this love? Possibly. It was never like this with Jason. I never feared losing him, not once during our ten years together. Yet, from the moment I looked up and saw Rhys sitting opposite me at Molly D's, I felt like there was a string that connected us. One that had absolutely nothing to do with Cupid or that app or...anything other than...*us*.

"Please stay with me."

Rhys must hear the note of panic in my voice and see the tears that slip from my eyes to spill down my flushed cheeks. He buries his hand in my hair, fisting the long strands, tugging only hard enough to force me to tilt my head to look at his face.

"Whatever happens at midnight is fated, Charlotte. We were always just along for the ride."

"Bullshit," I snap. I refuse to accept that a malicious winged cherub gets to decide our fate. "Do you want to stay?"

But what if he doesn't? What if Rhys prefers the void to me?

And therein lies my problem. The emotional abuse Jason inflicted left deep damage, and even now, in these last moments with this beautiful man, I can't let go of that ingrained cynicism.

"Of course I want to stay," Rhys growls. He shoves me away to gaze out the window. "You think I want to go back to that fucking place where I'm..." He flexes his hands, grasping at the air. "Where I'm nothing? Where the shape of your smile, and the golden flecks in your green eyes, and the sweet flavor of your body will haunt me until the last star swallows the last galaxy?" He turns back to me, and I see it in his eyes—the desperation festering in my heart reflected in his searching gaze. "But we were doomed to fail, Charlotte."

"What? What are you saying, Rhys? I don't understand."

His bitter laughter falls around us like drops of icy rain. "Cupid believes love conquers everything." He rakes his fingers through his messy, dark hair. Then, with a shake of his head, he adds, "But mortal hearts don't work that way. Your hearts are complicated. That's the beauty of you, Charlotte. Your tragedy. Your complexity. All the intricacies that make you unique. That's what Cupid can't manipulate with his"—he makes air quotes—"arrow."

I grab his wrist and slowly twist his hand. Blinking away fresh tears, I kiss his upturned palm. I keep hold of him, clutching his arm to my chest as if I can keep him here by sheer force of will. "Please don't go."

"We'll be okay, Charlotte."

"I'm sorry, Rhys. Oh, God, I'm so sorry."

"You have nothing to apologize for." He wipes away my tears before brushing his lips across mine. "Don't waste our last moments together like this."

Shaking my head, I lie right to his beautiful face. "I won't."

Inside, though, I'm screaming, crying, and begging Cupid to allow Rhys to stay, even as he's slipping through my fingers like sand. His connection to me is fading more with each passing second. But Rhys kisses me, his mouth a frantic distraction.

"I will never regret these days we spent together." Rhys murmurs against the frenzied pulse on the side of my throat. "Fucking never."

With my arms wrapped tight around Rhys's body, the heavy and frenetic beat of his heart resonates against my chest. "I'll bring you back. I swear it on my life."

But even as I make this promise, I drift off into the deepest sleep.

The blackest sleep.

The coldest sleep.

And the loneliest sleep I've ever known.

TWENTY-ONE

The emptiness hits even before I open my eyes.
I'm alone.
But I've been alone before.

The morning after my parents died, I woke up on Gram's couch, and I understood what it meant to be alone despite her being in the next room. When I went to school the following week, I was still alone, even though I was surrounded by people. It's a spiritual loneliness rather than a physical one. It's standing among humanity without connecting to a single soul.

I lie in bed, a hand pressed to my chest as my heart shatters beneath my sternum. But I can rot here all morning, and when I slowly sit up and push the riot of tangled curls away from my face, I meet the new day angry. Resentful. I sneer at the sunlight

spilling in through the open curtains. How dare the dawn arrive cheerful as fuck? How *dare* it not be gray and miserable outside when everything inside me is…dead?

I reach out to touch the mattress, sliding my hands across the empty place where Rhys lay only hours ago. I claw at the sheets where he slept. Gathering the blanket to hold it to my nose and inhale his lingering scent. Then I curse Cupid for taking him from me.

For stealing him like the cruelest of thieves.

God of Love, my ass.

"Fuck you," I snarl, punching the mattress. "Fuck you. Fuck you. Fuck you," I scream. "Bring him back, you fucking jerkoff," I demand, but then I rethink my strategy. Probably not the best idea to insult the deity who holds the key to Rhys's freedom. "No, wait, I'm sorry. Bring him back, *please*."

Nothing.

There's not even a ripple in the air or a whisper of Rhys's tantalizing baritone to break the silence. It's me here, alone, ruined, in this god-awful quiet. In this bed, in this house. While he's…

There.

Trapped in the void.

It's not fair. It's not right, and when I kick off the blanket, I want to rip my heart out and put it in the fucking blender. Anything would be better than living with it beating heavy but hollow, aching for something—someone—I can't have.

Needing to get as far away from my house as possible, away from where Rhys and I spent our last moments together, I swing my legs off the bed and snatch my phone off the nightstand. Torturing myself, I open The Book Boyfriends app, expecting…

I'm not sure what.

Maybe nothing. Or everything. Rhys to pop out, to knock on my door again. Or Cupid waiting for me, ready to chastise me for failing big-time. But…nothing. It's exactly as it was when I initially downloaded it.

"You made your point. Okay?" I swipe around, with every area now available to me as if I never matched with Rhys. When I go to the Contact page, I stare at it for a long, pregnant moment, wondering if I should…

If it will do a damn thing.

If anyone will even…

Screw it. Why not? What harm will it do at this point?

I type Cupid a message.

I messed up. Please don't make Rhys pay for my bullshit.

Simple, sure, but hopefully effective.

See, the thing is, I held instalove—or whatever we had—in the palm of my hands. Rather than see it for the gift Cupid gave me, I crushed it in my fist. Pulverized it and let it blow away. Rhys would be here if I hadn't been so goddamn afraid of getting hurt again. If I hadn't been so fucking stubborn. I'd have taken that leap of faith.

Look at what I cost us.

Rhys is gone—unmade and lost in that fucking void—and after I trudge to the bathroom with my guilt burdening each step I take, I hate the woman who stares back at me from the mirror as I brush my teeth. This miserable stranger with her curls in a riot and her sunken and haunted green eyes. I press my trembling fingertips to my lips, the ghost of Rhys's kiss lingering.

But for how long?

How long until I forget his lips pressed against mine or the slide of his hands along my body? When will his voice fade from my memory? Or will his striking face fade into a lost dream—same as my parents? Pushed somewhere to the back of my mind, too far for me to reach?

Oh, God...

My knees buckle, and I bury my face in my hands, with the blackness behind my eyes nothing compared to Rhys's prison. His unending nightmare. Although I push to my feet and strip off my clothes, I'm numb to the actions, moving by rote. A quick shower hides my tears, and after, I dress in a stupor, pulling on the only black dress I own—the one I bought in case of a funeral. I slip on my Doc Martens and grab my wallet, keys, and cell phone, but one step outside, into the fresh air, suffocates me. Somehow, I muster the fortitude to make the drive to The Scorched Page, glad for Brooklyn's company. My friend is a pleasant distraction, allowing me to pretend—for a little while, at least—that Rhys Ravenstone didn't dig himself deep into my heart.

That it took me exactly one week to fall wildly, madly, and impossibly in love with him.

"Charly!"

The snap of Brooklyn's fingers directly in front of my face wakes me out of my daze. I immediately straighten my wrist, leveling the limp mug in my hand. That was close. Another inch or two and coffee would have spilled onto the counter. "Huh? What's up?"

"Nothing," Brooklyn says, her expression peculiar as she watches me. "You okay?"

Nodding, I blink as if that will erase the flawless image of Rhys from my mind. "I'm fine. Why?"

Brooklyn points to the haphazardly shelved books I literally shoved into place before. "For starters, that mess. You treat every book like a treasure, so what's up with that? Then there's..." She waves her hands, gesturing at my unseasonably heavy, drab dress. "The mourning attire." She scrunches up her face. "Aw, man, Charly, did you and that hot dude break up already?"

I slam the mug on the counter. "Rhys is an off-limits subject."

"So, that's yes," Brooklyn remarks with the smugness that comes with knowing me better than anyone else other than Gram.

"Wrong," I counter. Technically, I'm not lying. Rhys and I never dated, and we certainly didn't break up.

Cupid took him.

Big difference.

Brooklyn strolls behind the counter and lays her arm over my shoulders. She gives me a light jostle, her floral-scented perfume swirling around us. "Well, if you need someone to talk to about your non-breakup, I'm here." She slides her arm off me and leans her hip against the counter. "We're besties. You can tell me anything."

I want to tell her the truth about Rhys. Oh, God, how I want to tell her, and when the words whisper from my lips, I let them flow again, like before, unable—*unwilling*—to stop them. "Hypothetically, let's say I didn't meet Rhys on Tinder."

Brooklyn's brows shoot up. "Okay...?"

"But let's also hypothetically say I found him on an app."

She goes to the coffee station to make a cup of tea and asks, "What's the name of this hypothetical app?"

"The Book Boyfriends," I answer with a cringe because it's preposterous.

She sets the bottle down, nodding. "Interesting."

"I'm serious," I deadpan.

"You hooked up with Rhys on a book boyfriend dating app? Big whoop," she retorts with a shrug. "Who the hell am I to judge? Lord knows I've had my fair share of embarrassing hookups. At least Rhys was fine as fuck. Some of mine were…" She feigns a shiver of disgust.

"No, Brooklyn, you don't understand." I pull out my phone and show her the app. Show her it's owned by Cupid and how a user can create a book boyfriend. "See? I built him. I built my ideal antihero, and at exactly midnight that same night, Rhys Ravenstone knocked on my front door."

Brooklyn pushes my hand away. "Come on, Charly, seriously?"

"I swear to God." I shove the phone at her. "I built him on here. Cupid gave us seven days to fall in love, but I fucked up, Brooklyn, because I fell in love with Rhys. I just didn't know it, and now he's gone, and there's no way for him to come back."

Maybe the anguish in my voice or the steady flow of tears convinces her that what I'm saying is true. Or perhaps she believes *I* believe it, and right now, that's enough, especially when she plucks the phone from my hand and sets it on the counter before wrapping her arms around me. I need her comfort, her support.

"Please don't cry."

"He's gone, Brooklyn," I sob. "He's gone, and it's my fault."

"You'll bring him back, Charly. If anyone can pull off a miracle, it's you." Then she sets me at arm's length, her laughter light. "But, girl, you have to know this is wild."

"Do you think I'm not aware of how crazy this sounds?" I ask. Of course, I am, and if it were her saying this to me, I'd assume she went full mental.

"Thank God you have yourself a bestie who believes in this crazy sort of shit." She pulls me back in for a quick, tight hug and laughingly says, "I'm the one who saw a UFO, remember? I'm the girl who goes to mediums and believes in the yeti and all that wild crap. But if you tell me you built yourself a real-life book boyfriend, then I guess you built yourself a real-life book boyfriend."

"Exactly!" I exclaim. Then, with a relieved, deflated sigh, I confess, "You have no idea how hard it was not to tell you about him the other day."

"I can imagine. And oh, my Lord, Charly, that man is blazing hot." Brooklyn fans herself. "I knew there was something unnatural about him."

"Remind me to tell you how Rhys made Jason piss his pants on the Fourth of July."

"Liar!" she says with a scandalized gasp. "He did not."

I make a cross over my heart. "He surely did." Then I get serious real quick. "I have to get him back, Brooklyn. He can't stay in that void, and I..." I drag in a deep breath, my heart aching. "I can't imagine life without him."

Brooklyn's wistful smile is positively lovely, brightening my best friend's pretty face. "You really do love him, don't you?"

"With everything I am."

Brooklyn tucks my hair behind my ear. "Then you'll find a way," she whispers.

A week ago, I learned that magic is real. Miracles happen. But I'm also a realist. A god gave me a gift, and what did I do? I shit on his generosity. Now, I hope to convince him to give me a second chance.

Somehow.

If I can figure out a way to get Cupid to even listen to me.

TWENTY-TWO

"Do you believe in instant love?" I ask casually, nonchalantly, but leave it to Gram to see right through my bullshit.

We're at the kitchen table, picking at our steak and salad for entirely different reasons. Gram's stomach issues prevent her from eating much anymore. As for me…

A broken heart doesn't make for a hearty appetite.

"For me, Muffin, or for you?"

Toying with the romaine speared on my fork, I shrug. "Both? Or just me. I don't know." I redirect my gaze to her, with my heart splintering even more. Today isn't a good day. Sure, she got a bath, with her gray hair in a tidy bun, and she's in a new blue house dress. But the hunch of her shoulders and the laborious breathing tell a terrible story. "Do you, though? Do you believe people can fall in love—*real* love—almost immediately?"

"Depends on the people," she counters before tucking a tiny square of steak between her wrinkled lips.

"Okay, fine. *Me*, Gram. Me. Do you think I can fall in instalove with someone?"

Gram swallows her bite of meat. "Sure, I do," she says, but is also quick to add, "When you're not busy being a stubborn ass."

"Gram!"

"Charly!" she shoots back at me. "Someone's got to tell you the facts before you lose that boy of yours."

The fork slips from my hand, dropping onto the plate. "I already lost him." I rest my elbows on the table and lean my chin on my hands, the hitch in my voice mirroring the tears I'm holding back.

"So, get him back," she says, as if it were that easy.

Utterly defeated, I shake my head and clasp my hands in my lap. "I can't."

"Bullshit. Yes, you can."

With my eyes downcast, I whisper, "I can't, Gram. Rhys is *gone*—forever gone."

"Oh, Muffin, he's not dead, is he?"

The question whispers out of her mouth like poison sliding off her tongue. Neither of us deals well with death, for obvious reasons. I lost my parents, true, but Millie Benson buried her only child. That a giant 'fuck you' to the natural order of life. The cruelest thing the universe can do to a parent. Even the word 'death' is still difficult for her to say. And who would blame her for it? Not me. Not anyone with half a heart.

Yet Gram held my hand as best she could through my miscarriage, which, of course, resurfaced the agony of losing her daughter and son-in-law—whom she adored like he was her own child. She is an extraordinary woman whose strength is remarkable. But grief and ill health took their toll, and sitting across from her now, I realize how precious and fleeting her time left here is.

She, too, is slipping through my fingers.

"No, Gram, Rhys isn't dead."

He's alive—if having consciousness in that…*place*…is living.

She presses a hand to her breast, huffing out a breath of relief. "Oh, thank God. Charly! The way you said that. You had me worried there for a minute."

"But he's still gone, Gram, and where he went…" I let my sentence trail off, a lump leaping into my throat. "And I don't think he can ever come back."

"Where'd the boy go, fucking Mars?"

Leave it to Gram to make me laugh, but it's momentary. "He might as well be, and it's my fault. I could have kept him here, but I was too afraid to admit I love him because of what Jason did to me. I let all that bullshit ruin what I had with Rhys, and now he's gone, and I honestly don't know how I'm going to—"

"Charlotte Allison Mallory." Gram throws down her fork and lifts her chin defiantly. "I didn't raise you to be a quitter." She bangs her weathered hand on the table. "After I put your parents in the ground—God rest their souls—everyone told me to keep you out of school. Give you time to heal. Hell no. I got you dressed and sent you right back. You must have thought I was cruel, but I couldn't have you sitting around here all day and night, consumed by grief. I wanted you out there living. Don't you think I wanted to keep you with me? Safe? Right here where I could see you? But I knew I'd be cutting you off at the knees. Killing you but leaving you alive. Understand?" At my numb nod, Gram goes on, saying, "Oh, how you cried, Muffin, and I let you. Sure I did. I let you get out all those big emotions every time you needed that good cry. As soon as you were fine, though, I made you wash your face and made you get right back to living. Because I didn't want you to become me. I see what I did to myself. I gave up, Muffin, and I'll be damned if you're going to quit on life, too. If that man is gone, for whatever reason, and you want him back, you go find him, and if you can't, then you move on and get back to living."

I grip the edge of the table, whispering, "Gram…"

"No," she snaps. "Don't you *Gram* me. Tell me you understand, Muffin."

I nod, so sad for her. Sorry for the life she lost to grief. Furious at the driver who killed my parents. And I'm angry at myself for hurting Rhys because of my stubbornness to see what was right in front of my eyes since the moment he slid into the booth opposite me at Molly D's. "Okay."

"Okay, *what*?"

"Okay, I promise that if I can't bring Rhys back to Harley Cove, I won't give up on myself."

"That's my girl." Then Gram pushes away her plate, her food barely touched. "I don't have a lot of time left, and that's the truth. Don't let me leave here with a conflict weighing on me."

Miserable, scared of losing her, I shoot off the chair, and when I wrap my arms around her frail body, I hate, hate, hate how fragile she feels. "There's no conflict, Gram. I love you. Thank you for always knowing exactly what I need to hear."

She gives me a weak, reassuring pat. "That's what I'm here for, Muffin. And one day, you'll be the one knowing what to say to your kids to get them through a tough spot."

The idea of children is a punch to the gut, and one more reason I need to rescue Rhys from the void. Because when I envision a future, I only see him—us as a family. My antihero. If that meddling cherub really is the God of Love, then maybe… He'll take pity on us. Give us one more chance. One more shot at our happily ever after.

I kiss Gram on the cheek. "I have to go. Need anything before I leave?"

"For you to be happy."

I give her my best fake smile. "I will be, Gram. One way or the other, I will be, promise."

"That's all I want for you, Muffin." She cups my cheeks, her watery eyes searching mine. "Now, get your boy back, even if you have to go to Mars to do it."

Hell, I'll dive into the darkness and go find him, if that's what it'll take. Anything to bring him home to me…

Where he belongs.

TWENTY-THREE

*F*our *days.*
Four days' worth of research has yielded nothing.
Damnit.
Four days wasted.

Four days of Rhys still lost in darkness while I've been scouring the internet for something. Anything. Just to be right where I was four fucking days ago. No new information gained on The Book Boyfriends or how it can manifest people.

Weird.

A person can find literally anything about anything on the internet. It's actually shocking what I came across online. Some shit that made me want to pop out my eyeballs and wash them

with bleach. But you know what I didn't find? A damn thing about Cupid's app.

Apparently, it's like the first two rules of Fight Club.

1. You do not talk about The Book Boyfriends.
2. You do *not* talk about The Book Boyfriends.

And I totally get it, I do. Other than my super awesome best friend, few people would believe you can build a man on an app. Still, I find it odd that I've found no online chatter. Nothing—not a website or a download link. Nothing. Not a trace that this app exists anywhere except on my phone.

Oh, and it vanished from the app store.

For a hot second, I doubt it even happened. Maybe I imagined them? Was it a wild dream, and I made Rhys up in my mind? No, it happened, and Rhys Ravenstone was real.

That nagging voice of doubt? That's pre-Rhys Charlotte.

Post-Rhys Charlotte trusts in the unbelievable.

This new version of me believes in the impossible because the impossible knocked on my door and changed me for the better.

But after four days of finding absolutely nothing, I'm… disheartened. Of course, I'm not giving up. No, I'll keep pressing on, diving deeper into the dark web. What I find hilarious is that I've learned enough about Greek mythology and the gods' family tree that I could give a TED Talk on the subject.

Not that my newfound knowledge has helped.

On the couch, laptop open, surrounded by an eclectic mix of romance novels and books on mythology, I blow stray hair away from my face and pound the keyboard. Another empty search term that yields zero results.

Damnit.

I yank the spoon from the pint of strawberry ice cream (a sadly underrated flavor, in my humble opinion) that's on the coffee table, only to stab it back into the frozen deliciousness. I scoop out a hearty amount and shovel it in my mouth, wincing at the brain freeze that follows. The gulp of warm air I take to counter the cold helps as I chew, and after I swallow, I wonder out loud, "Where are you holding him prisoner, you miserable asshole?"

Currently, Cupid is at the top of my shit list.

I tap the spoon against my lips, thinking. Always thinking. My mind hasn't shut off since the morning I woke up alone.

I jab the spoon back in the ice cream before snatching my phone off the couch cushion. Opening The Book Boyfriends app, I check messages. Nothing. The one I sent remains unread. See? He's a little winged asshole. I hope he accidentally shoots one of those fucking arrows into his own foot.

To hell with it waiting.

I send another.

And another, flooding 'customer service' with about a billion messages.

"Let's see if you can ignore me now, dickhead."

The problem is that I don't know if these messages are going to an actual person—or possibly to the deity himself. Or anyone. For all I know, this page is bogus. But I have hope. And so, I send more. A ton more, until my goddamn thumbs hurt from the furious typing as I bare my entire soul in a series of rambling messages.

To Cupid.

To whoever might read these.

I write about how I was my grandmother's rock when she couldn't be strong for herself and how I maintained good grades in school despite…everything. That I did everything right, followed every rule, crossed every *t*, dotted every *i*, and even when life knocked me down, I got back up and kept fighting. I ramble on about how one of my greatest regrets is quitting college because I wanted to become a child psychologist. Most of all, I write about Rhys.

Wonderful, glorious, arrogant, selfless, Rhys Ravenstone.

Rhys could have easily been one-dimensional—an avatar—soulless and cruel. Instead, he was vibrant and alive. He blindsided me, stormed into my life and spun me upside down. It took less than a week for him to do the impossible—to shatter the wall around my heart and work his way into the fabric of my soul. No man I've ever known has been more worthy of love than Rhys Ravenstone.

My antihero.

I beg—*beg him*—to set Rhys free. To *please* let me right the wrong I did by not trusting in the gift he gave me. Because the moment Rhys knocked on my door, he changed everything. He became my everything.

I end the last message with a simple, *please send him home.*

After I hit Send, I toss aside the phone and lay my head on the back of the couch to stare up at the ceiling, my heart slamming against my sternum and tears raining down my cheeks.

I won't quit.

I won't *ever* quit.

Not until the last star swallows the last galaxy.

TWENTY-FOUR

"You seem better today."

Shocked by Brooklyn's observation, I snort out a laugh as I look up from the inventory sheet displayed on the screen of my laptop. "Really? Because I feel like shit."

Nine lonely, sleepless nights, with today being the tenth straight miserable day spent buried up to my eyeballs in research. I'm strung out, frayed at both ends, and about ready to snap at any moment. But I've kept the candle burning, and while I refuse to give up, I've run headfirst into nothing but brick walls.

"At least you stopped with the funeral garb."

She's exaggerating. I have one black dress, but okay, yes. I may have dusted off a few of my old emo-phase pieces, but I returned them to the closet. Today, I'm dressed more appropriately for the weather—tan cargo shorts paired with an orange knit tank top. I braided my curls. It's ungodly humid and I'm in no mood to play Fight the Frizz.

Part of not giving up is not letting myself go to shit—even though all I want to do is crawl into bed and wallow. But this little engine is going to keep trudging up the mountain. I won't stop until I rescue Rhys, and if that means hauling my ass out of bed each morning, taking a fucking shower, and putting in the work until the work is done and he's home, then that's what I have to do.

"Oh, I'm sorry, Miss It's Always Sunny in Harley Cove." The snark is heavy in my retort. "I remember a time not so long ago when you came to work looking like doom and gloom every day for *well* over a month."

"Ha, ha!" Brooklyn says sarcastically. "That was different."

"Yeah, why?"

Brooklyn lifts a short stack of new books and carries them toward a spot we made for them over in the paranormal romance section. "It was me, not you."

"Oh, my gawd," I drawl. "You totally have Main Character Syndrome."

"Hell yeah I do!" Brooklyn says, laughing, with a toss of her head that sends her strawberry-blond hair cascading over her shoulder.

"At least you know it," I call out, laughing.

The bell above the door chimes, and as always, hope flares. I swear my heart skips a beat, and I get breathless and lightheaded, wishing—hoping, praying—it's Rhys who's walking inside The

Scorched Page. But that hope dies a swift death when it's Lisa who hesitantly enters.

Fuck me.

As always, she looks as fresh as the summer breeze. Bold move for her to walk her floral-dress-wearing ass into my bookshop as if my...*Rhys*...didn't threaten to skin Jason alive and hang him on a meat hook less than two weeks ago. But here she is, and when she waves to Brooklyn, my bestie gives her the ol' up-and-down shifty eye without returning the friendly greeting.

Lisa offers me an awkward smile. "Hi, Charly."

"Lost?" I drawl.

Again, she glances at Brooklyn, and my gawd, how I love my friend for this. Brooklyn throws Lisa the single most sarcastic glare in the history of glares right before flipping Jason's fiancée the finger. I wink at her and give her a little shake of the head, silently calling her off. Brooklyn rolls her eyes, clearly unhappy that she can't antagonize the woman.

"Can we talk?" Lisa asks, her discomfort palpable. Fucking good. "Please?"

Curious despite myself, I close the laptop, giving the stunning blonde my undivided attention. "Sure. Why not? This should be good."

Brooklyn jabs her thumb toward the front door. "I'm, uh... Guess it's a good time for me to take my break, huh?"

I fish my wallet out of my bag and grab some cash. "Here. We've been busting to try the new coffee shop on the corner of Cain and Pawn. Why don't you grab us something?" As much as I hate to ask, I turn to Lisa. "Want something?"

She's pregnant, and I'm not rude.

Taken aback, she shakes her head. "No, thank you, though."

"Whatever." Then to Brooklyn, "Only for us, then. Surprise me."

Brooklyn takes the cash. "You got it, babe." She eyeballs Lisa again before saying to me, "I'm a phone call away if you need me."

"Thanks, but I'll be fine."

As she walks out, I glance at Lisa and shrug before slapping my hands against my thighs. "Okay, so, what? What do you want to talk about? Something specific or, like, a general conversation? Because I can play nice and do either."

With a sigh, Lisa places her white designer purse on the counter. When she tightens her ponytail, I cringe in sympathy at the headache it must cause. I remember the days when I was with Jason, and the pressure to be perfect was slowly killing me. Immaculate appearance, irreproachable behavior. Never a hair out of place. Never raise my voice. Fake every orgasm lest I bruise my husband's fragile ego.

No wonder I built an antihero.

I craved excitement. The thrill of being with someone who would breathe life back into me after a decade of trying—and failing—to live as a fucking Stepford Wife.

"Something specific." Lisa smooths her hands down her dress, and I realize she has a baby bump. Her flared dresses hide it, but it *is* there, and instead of resentment, I'm happy for her. Better her than me tied to that asshole for the rest of her life. "I told you I owe you an apology. I wanted to wait a bit until things… settled…before coming to see you. Now that they have, I need you to know that I'm truly sorry for the hurt I caused you. I accept your hatred and understand if you can never forgive me."

I should hate her. She and I weren't exactly friends, but we knew each other. Knew each other well enough that Girl Code applied. I would have never slept with her husband if the situation had been reversed. But I'm also the sort of woman who would never be a man's mistress. I could never stab a fellow woman in the back. Women aren't my enemies or my competition. And honestly, my marriage might as well have been a million years ago. I don't love Jason, and after Rhys, I wonder if I ever did. I'm holding on to anger for the sake of being angry. For the sake of having a bruised ego, not because I actively give a shit.

And that's why I mean it when I say, "I don't hate you."

Lisa is visibly relieved. Her entire body relaxes as she exhales a slow sigh. "Thank you."

I snort out a laugh. "Don't thank me. Jason's your problem now. You get to deal with his bullshit until death do you part. Good fucking luck."

Lisa chews her bottom lip a moment before confessing, "I thought that man was going to kill Jason."

That man.

Rhys.

"Truth?"

She nods. "Truth."

"For a minute there, I did as well." I lift a single brow, mimicking Rhys perfectly. "Between us girls, I wonder how sad you'd be if he had."

"Charly!" Lisa gasps, but her frown magically turns upside down. In fact, her blue eyes come alive with mischief. This is the most animated I've seen her since... Well, before she hooked up with my ex-husband. He changed her. "That's awful."

"Awful that I said it, or awful that, for a second, you hoped he'd have done it."

She's silent for too long. Long enough for me to think she won't answer. But then she whispers, "Both."

"Glad to see Jason hasn't sucked all the life out of you. Yet. Don't let him." I tap my temple. "Don't let the Wembleys mess with your mind. Twisting you into knots. Just… Those people are goddamn vultures, every one of them. First, they'll kill your spirit, then they'll peck at what's left of you. Be careful, that's all I'm saying."

She's already nodding. "I will."

"Good." And I hope she will, for no other reason than to protect that baby from that awful family. "It must have been difficult to come here. I'm glad you did."

Again, she fidgets with her ponytail. "You're very intimidating," she admits.

"Me?" I exclaim.

"Yes, you. Look at what you've accomplished, Charly." She spins, gesturing to the bookshop. "Like you said, the Wembleys are vultures. They tried to break you, but they couldn't. You're thriving. In one year, you bought your own home. Opened your own business. You blossomed into your own person. I admire you." With a hand resting on her tiny bump, she turns back to me, and my God, she looks despondent. "My greatest regret is that you and I can never be friends because of what I did to you."

I step out from behind the counter and take her hands, giving them a gentle squeeze. "We're not enemies, and that's a start."

"Maybe we can go for lunch one day?"

"Yeah, no. Not there yet." I drop her hands, and she looks crestfallen. "But I do like ice cream."

Lisa perks up, her eyes brightening. "I won't say no to a chocolate-dipped cone."

"Guess we have a playdate, then."

"Guess we do," she says.

And just like that, the giant chip on my shoulder falls away, leaving me lighter than I've felt in a long time.

TWENTY-FIVE

My laughter is bittersweet as I plop down onto the couch, bowl of popcorn in hand. It's impossible not to think about the night Rhys knocked on my door or the day after we went food shopping. Such a mundane activity—but one I'd give up a kidney to do with him again.

I miss him.

God, how I miss him.

Miserable, I toss a handful of popcorn in my mouth, chewing through a smile, laughing over how he asked if I wanted corn or carrots, and I thought he asked if I wanted porn.

With a *P*.

Not corn with a *C*.

Was it ten days ago?

No, it had to be a lifetime ago. A million years and a million tears ago.

I grab my laptop and shove aside the dread that comes with knowing I'll hit yet another brick wall. But maybe tonight will be different. I hope. I hope, I hope, I hope as my fingers hover over the keyboard and I stare at the empty search bar, not knowing what term to put there.

What word haven't I tried?

What could I have possibly missed?

My phone pings, and because it's late—almost midnight—I immediately check it to see if it's Gram. God forbid. She'd only text if something were wrong. Wait, no. It's a direct message.

From The Book Boyfriends.

Oh my fucking God.

My hand trembles and my fingers fumble as I open the app, and there it is, bold as you please. Admin has replied to my messages. With my heart pounding so damn hard it actually hurts and my blood rushing so fast, I'm a little dizzy. I tap the little notification envelope and I land at the message center, and there—*right there*—is a note.

For me.

From Cupid.

Dear Charlotte Mallory (Member #822),

Thank you for reaching out to The Book Boyfriends on behalf of Rhys Ravenstone. I appreciate the time it took for you to send a disturbing number of messages pleading his case. While I understand you feel I've been most unfair by "ripping him away" to send him back to that "miserable fucking void," I assure you I afforded you the same opportunity I give to every broken soul I encounter. You failed to believe in true love until it was too late. However, after carefully reviewing the many (and often rambling and incoherent) messages, I may reconsider my judgment on two conditions. Answer the below question honestly (I'll know if you're lying) and I'll let you know the second condition.

Do you love Rhys Ravenstone?

—Cupid, aka "cruel motherfucker" "dickhead" and "asshole"

I can barely see past the tears welled in my eyes. I don't even know how I'm typing, but somehow, my fingers find the right keys.

Yes. I am madly, wildly, undeniably in love with Rhys Ravenstone. Please let him come home to me.

After hitting Send, I slide off the couch, my knees hitting the carpet. Wedged in the narrow space between the coffee table and the couch, I press the phone to my forehead. "Please, please, please. Cupid, please."

I repeat this for what feels like hours, but it's minutes at most when my phone pings again. Tapping the app, I see another reply.

Dear Charlotte Mallory (Member #822),
Correct answer.
*Second condition: The Book Boyfriends is exactly like Fight Club. I picked you for a reason. Now that you're part of our shared secret, you will keep our secret. Yeah, yeah, I know you told your friend. She won't remember it. I'm a god, remember? I giveth, and I can taketh away. *wink**

—Cupid, aka "the happily ever after maker"

I blow out a breath, but when I try to reply, I can't. The app won't let me type. It keeps flashing 'error,' and when I click out of it and return to the main screen of my cell phone... Panicking, I let out a small cry when I see the one fragile line of communication I had with Cupid—the only connection with Rhys—is gone. The app is deleted off my phone, and when I hear the rain start, I push off my knees and...

What?

What am I supposed to do now?

Wait? For what?

"I do love him," I whisper. "I swear to you, I love Rhys Ravenstone right down to the crumbs of him."

Midnight comes.

The knock has me gasping, nearly jumping out of my skin. With an excited squeal, I toss my phone on the couch before dashing for the door. But I skid to a halt, frozen for a moment, terrified this is a twisted joke, as I stare at his unmistakable outline through the smoked glass.

Him.

Tall, wide, and powerful him.

My antihero.

"Charlotte Mallory?" The deep rumble on the other side of the locked door is *very* male and *very* calm.

"Who's asking?" I, on the other hand, am a fucking wreck.

"Rhys Ravenstone." His palm flattens against the glass. "Open the door."

I slap a trembling hand over my mouth. Curl my sweaty hand around the knob, and the moment I swing it open, Rhys storms inside, forcing me to leap backward.

"You're here."

He fills all the space in the room. Absorbs all the air, and when he reaches for me, I back up again, not trusting myself to touch him. Afraid he'll crumble to dust beneath my hands. "Cupid rarely changes his mind. What the hell did you say to him?"

"Everything," I breathe. I drag my gaze over him, from the top of his disheveled dark hair to his wet, black clothes, down to the heavy boots, and back to his perfect, chiseled face. "I told him everything."

He narrows those eyes on me. "Be specific, Charlotte."

I watch him follow the trail of my tongue as I lick my lips. Then I notch my chin and leap right off a cliff. "I love you, Rhys Ravenstone. I love you, and it's okay if you don't love me back. I'll hate it and be miserable for the rest of my life, but I'll deal with it somehow. I can't live with you being trapped in that void."

And I think that's what love is, right? You put their happiness and well-being above your own—even if it breaks your heart. If Rhys rejects me, I'll shatter into a million pieces right here, right now, at his feet. But I'll still let him go because anything is better than his suffering.

"Come here to me, Charlotte." Chills break out across my flesh at how he crooks his finger at me, beckoning me. Rhys has seen every inch of me. We've done things I never even *thought* to do with another living soul. But here I am, in a long, pink T-shirt and socks, suddenly super self-conscious as I inch toward him. When I'm within arm's reach, he grabs me, pulling me against his body, his rain-soaked clothes wetting me. Locking me in his arms. He nods at the front door. "You'll be good if I walk out right now?"

My mouth tastes like ash, and my limbs are heavy and numb. "Do you want to?"

"Answer the fucking question."

"If that's what you want, then yes."

"Liar."

"All you've known is a prison. Now that you're free, I won't put you in a different set of shackles."

Rhys kisses my forehead. "Your brain has to hurt from the nonsense that swirls around in there." He kisses the tip of my nose. "How can you see yourself as a shackle, Charlotte?"

"I'm giving you your freedom."

Up goes that single brow. "You can't gift me something that was never yours to give. Cupid owned my soul. I could have gone anywhere after he pulled me from the void."

Confused, I say, "But you came here."

"Curiosity compelled me to knock on your door." He releases me to smooth his palms over my curls. Run them over my shoulder and down my sides, settling his hands on the curve of my hips. "I stayed because of you."

I rise on my tiptoes and brush my lips over his. "Thank you for knocking on my door, Rhys, twice."

"Thank you for loving me, Charlotte."

"That was my pleasure."

"Damn right, it is." He sweeps me off my feet. "You know I love you."

Laughing, I say, "Now I do."

"I love the hell out of you, Charlotte. The void, the darkness, that wasn't torture. Being separated from you was unbearable."

I press my palm to his cheek. "I hated every second we were apart."

He releases a long exhale, a scowl fixed on his face. "When you pieced me together, you did a hell of a job, sweetheart. You gave me some serious fucked up inclinations."

"You've done fine so far." I rise on my tiptoes and kiss him. "The rest, we'll figure out."

"That we will." He sweeps me off my feet, literally. "I missed you."

"I missed you, too." I bite the inside of my cheek, then ask, "This is crazy. Like, what do we do now? What's first?"

He nods at the top of the stairs, carrying me toward them. "First, I fuck you because I can't wait much longer to get inside you." We reach the top landing. "And tomorrow, we start the rest of our lives."

"Sounds like the perfect plan to me."

I wish my parents could have met Rhys. I wish they could see me happy. To see I'm loved and safe. After so many years, the details of them have faded from my mind, becoming a faded dream. But I think they would have liked him. I *hope* they would have liked him. My dad would have gotten a kick out of him because he is protective of me. And my mom… She would have loved how sweet he is beneath his ferocious exterior.

The same man who threatened to skin Jason is the same person who lays me on the bed and covers me with his body. He kisses every inch of me, demanding nothing. Gives everything. Holds my heart as if it's the most precious treasure in all the world. Allows me a level of control over him no one else on this earth will ever have. And when he roars my name, and I cry out his, I finally understand what 'forever' means. Because with Rhys, that's what we have—a forever love…

Signed, sealed, and delivered by Cupid himself.

THE END

ACKNOWLEDGMENTS

Frankie, thank you for your enthusiasm while I wrote this. You knew I couldn't retire! If I had this app, I'd build you right down to the silver in your goatee. I love so damn much!

Brooklyn Cross, my MVP. My best friend. I love you. Thank you for talking me out of retirement. You are…everything. You make this whole thing fun. I'd be incomplete without you.

Molly Doyle, you're adorable, and I adore you. Each time we talk, you shine on my day like sunshine.

Nikki St. Crowe, you are the sweetest badass to ever touch a keyboard. Thank you for the world you've created, the characters we love, and the person you are.

Harley Laroux, you're such a lovely soul, a true blessing upon this world. Thank you for the hours of escape your books gave me when life was at its most chaotic.

Mandy, you live in a special corner of my heart. It was as if the universe put us together right when we needed each other.

Thank gawd we met. I'd be lost without your beautiful smile and musical laughter.

Taylor, I love you. It really is as simple as that. I'm counting down the days until we finally get to be silly together in person. The only problem is, I'm not going to let you go!

Wren, Brianna, and Hollie, thank you for being the first to read Charlotte and Rhys's story. Without you, they wouldn't be here, out in the wild. I'm so grateful for your time and all you've done to make this book happen!

Patreons, thank you for sticking with me. It's been a rough ride, and I'm sorry for that, but only smooth days ahead!

Rebels, thank you for keeping the conversation going and being so awesome! We're a small but fantastic group, and I appreciate each of you!

Readers, oh, my gawd, you are the best. Seriously. I was on the verge of retiring. In fact, I made a soft announcement to friends and family, intending to drift away quietly. But word got out, and some of you wrote to me, begging me not to stop writing. Your kind words helped encourage me to give it one more go. Well, I'm still here. Because of you. I adore you, and I'm so grateful for your support!

ABOUT RENEE ROCCO

Renee Rocco writes complex antiheroes, pairing them with tormented heroines. She's always enjoyed exploring the darker side of her imagination and finally found peace in Contemporary/Dystopian Dark Romance and Dark Romantasy.

Hidden behind the glamour of work-from-home mom duties, Renee is a suburban misfit who always has a sarcastic comment at the ready—whether the situation calls for one or not. A former Brooklynite who migrated to the infamous Jersey Shore, she's rarely Instagram-ready or speakerphone-friendly. She also shamelessly abuses the em dash and ellipsis and suffers from an iced coffee addiction.

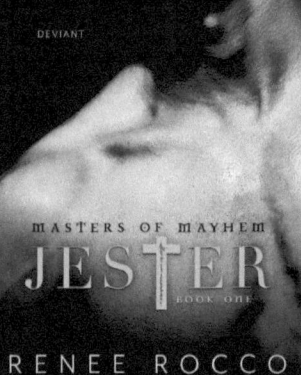

Nice women aren't supposed to enjoy filthy sex with bad men.

THE GRIM TOWER DUET

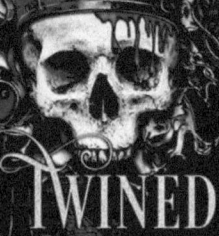

Forget what you've read. There is no Prince Charming in this fairy tale.

www.ingramcontent.com/pod-product-compliance
Lightning Source LLC
LaVergne TN
LVHW041811060526
838201LV00046B/1217